LUCIA

~Novel~

Corinne Wandenburg

For those who loved till death and beyond!
To a strong and delicate woman : Claudia Popovici !

Infarom Publishing
office@infarom.com
www.infarom.com

ISBN: 978-973-1991-60-3

Publisher: **INFAROM**
Author: **Corinne Wandenburg**
Translator: **Maria Letiția Chiculiță**
Correction editor: **CarolAnn Johnson**
Cover design: **Liping Wang**
Original title: *Lucia* (Romanian)

PART I

CHAPTER 1

One beautiful summer morning, perfect for a ride in a carriage, when the whole of nature was striving to please the world, a messenger dripping with sweat stopped his horse at the door of Count de Sousa y Monterro's castle. One could tell that he had finally reached his destination.

He knocked at the impressive doors and since he was expected, the doors opened immediately.

"Good day! Is the Count home?" the messenger asked.

"Yes," the servant answered, "he is waiting for you! This way, please! Are you Dom Miguel Ribeiro?"

"In the flesh! My horse needs immediate attention!"

"Someone will look after him, do not worry about that."

Dom Miguel Ribeiro followed the count's servant through a dreamlike décor. Spiral stairs, floral arangement crafted by skilled gardeners, artesian wells pouring their water into basins full of exotic fish.

The Sousa y Monterro Castle had belonged to the family for centuries. They had always taken pride in that. On the castle door, there had endured for centuries the coat of arms of the family: two crested aigrettes on the bank of a river, delicate yet merciless, and below them was the dictum "MODESTIS SED IMPORTUNUS." From the very entrance, the extraordinary, imposing building revealed its importance. It was a sturdy, permanently occupied construction, upon which time had not yet left its imprint. The recent renovations spoke for themselves. Behind the castle was a lovely park which we will have the chance to talk about later.

Dom Miguel Ribeiro followed the servant to a room where he was asked to wait. He took a seat, exhausted after his journey. He was a robust, chunky man, and not very tall. He was around thirty years old. But though his physique was not all he would have wanted, it was compensated by his acute expression, tall forehead, and well-shaped mouth.

The room in which he waited was a sort of study of the Count. There, the Count received people from his domain who had come on various business concerns and issues at the castle. The Count was seen as a kind and just man, so he had set aside a few days to receive visitors, so that the good order of the household should not be disturbed – which would trouble Doña Alba, his wife, who would lift her hands above her head, leaving without uttering a single word.

Very soon, the Count appeared in the doorway.

"Dom Miguel, it's so good to finally see you again. I do hope that the people who sent you are in good health and convey good news to me."

Dom Miguel bowed in respect and replied:

"The Baron de Cantarra is well, and so is his entire family. He sends you many good wishes from Lisbon. He also wishes you much good health and sends you this letter, to which he expects an answer." Thereupon, the baron's envoy took from his chest a thick envelope with a wax seal showing the baron's stamp, and then bowed low, as if to make room for the Count for his reading.

"It seems," the Count said, "that the baron trusted only his dear and faithful Dom Miguel Ribeiro to bring this letter! You are worthy to take back my answer. But I will not write it down. We are still living odd times, and I do not dare to. Dom Rui Alfonso de Cantarra says you are always praised for your merits. So I kindly ask you to tell the Baron that I, Count Filipe de Sousa y Monterro, shall give him the hand of my daughter Lucia, for his son Pedro, with my blessing! May this union bind our common interests even further and may no one break them."

Dom Miguel replied, "This is the news that my master and friend is waiting for. Still, you should consider writing a letter, even a short one, regarding a date for the announcement."

"Ah, yes, you are right!" The Count rang a bell, and a servant came in shortly. "Please see Dom Miguel Ribeiro to a guest room, and remain at his disposal!" He turned to Dom Miguel: "I suppose you will not turn down a night in my castle! You will meet Lucia, my daughter, tonight over dinner. You can then describe her better to the Baron."

"Thank you for your hospitality," the guest said, following the servant. "I shall wait for that letter in the morning."

"You will have it; now get some rest!"

CHAPTER 2

I kindly ask the reader to forgive us if we entered too abruptly into the topic of our story. It would have been appropriate to describe first the family of this nobleman of Portugal. But, with apologies, we will do so now.

The wealthy family from Santa Cruz, a town nearby Coimbra, had ruled over its lands since the time when Coimbra was the capital. Dom Felipe was a tall, good-looking man. He belonged to that class of people who remain charming all their lives. He was a just, kind man, not over fifty. He had married Doña Alba, his cousin, who was five years younger than he. In his youth, she had been quite a conquest for him. His wife was still beautiful even at the age of forty-five. But the paintings showing her in her youth told it all: she was a perfect beauty. She had splendid long, black hair, which she wore according to the fashion of the time. Her lips were soft and red, and her skin was ivory and silky. As for her eyes.... They held a fire that would melt any attempt to resist or to fight. She had had many suitors, but on her parents' advice, she had agreed to marry in the family, to her cousin. Had she loved anyone else before her marriage, only she and the good God knew that. She never opposed the marriage, but then again her heart did not leap with delight as it should have. She just took this union as a duty. Her parents had talked her into such a marriage, for Alba was their only child.

Dom Felipe was pleased, proud, and enchanted when Doña Alba became his fiancée. Her beauty had put a spell on him. Their marriage had been celebrated with great splendor less than one year after their engagement, and the new bride followed her husband to the old castle under the seal of the two aigrettes. She did not regret a thing. She had lived a peaceful life with the usual duties of the wife of a nobleman who also owned a domain, a province in the countryside.

When children came, she became more active. Motherhood had changed her, had helped her mature, but her face and body remained just as beautiful. Dom Felipe was pleased to have a heir, Francisco. Obviously,

5

he loved his beautiful daughter as well, but she "would get married anyway and leave home, while a son…."

Francisco acquired his mother's beauty and his father's acuity. Lucia looked like her father, but after she grew up, everyone noticed a certain melancholy about her that made her quiet. She was a kind but invisible beauty. She spent most of her time in her room with her nanny who had raised both her and her brother. When she went for a walk, she did so only in the park of the castle. There was a significant age difference between Lucia and Francisco. She was only sixteen; her brother was twenty-five. Things did change a bit when she received as a gift a small horse, which she would ride every day on the bank of the Mondego River.

The relationship between the two children was one full of love, even though they were different in nature. Francisco had an optimistic spirit and was always joking; his smile hardly ever left his lips. He was able to make Lucia come out of her shell and hold her interest with his stories about the capital.

Whenever he came back from Lisbon, he would bring her either a special bird in a cage or feminine trinkets, which made Lucia very happy. It seemed that Francisco's life was active, but not scandalous. He was a wealthy young man who was sometimes allowed to do naughty things. He was handsome and easygoing, so doors were opened to him.

When he would start telling Lucia stories, it was as if she lived them together with her brother, who had gone away to study. They wrote long letters to each other, and Francisco confessed his innermost thoughts to his sister without fearing he would be betrayed. And now, the young man's return during the holidays was eagerly anticipated. He had finally finished his naval studies, which had taken quite some years, to the unhappiness of people wanting him home.

Thus, the description of this family may end here. They were contented together in the peace of the castle, and if they were not, they hid it very well.

CHAPTER 3

Doña Alba came down from her room to the library with her ever-present knitting basket. She hoped she would find Lucia there. She had looked for her in her room, but the girl wasn't there. Momentarily distracted, Lucia had left the door to the canary's cage open. That was a careless thing to do, and it would have cost her dearly, for the window was wide open. Fortunately, her mother simply closed the door to the cage so the canary was safe, and Lucia could continue to enjoy his songs.

In the library, she found her beloved daughter with a book in her hand, but not reading it. She was again caught in that melancholia that caused her not to hear or see a thing. She was an innocent child, a kind and pure virgin. A piece of clay that her mother was molding in her hands.

Doña Alba knew her goal. Her husband had ordered her to talk to Lucia about a prospective marriage. That marriage was to serve the family's interests and should not be refused. Doña Alba sat down next to Lucia, who was startled.

"Mother, my dear mother!"

"What are you doing here with the book in your hands and your eyes far away? I looked for you in your room – the door to the canary cage was open – what are you dreaming about, my sweet angel?"

"I'm thinking about Francisco. He will be home soon. He wrote to me, promising me long trips together. He also promised me presents when we see each other again, and visits to Coimbra. I'm waiting for him. When he is here, I feel alive. He teaches me so much!"

"My darling, life does not stand still. Sooner or later, you will get married. In fact, this is what I wanted to talk to you about. Your father wishes me to tell you about an arrangement in this respect...."

"Married?" Lucia said, in astonishment "I am not ready at all to leave you! I have all the time in the world. I am only sixteen!"

"This is a wonderful age, my dear!"

"But I do not want this now! I still want to play, to walk in our beloved park. Marriage... I don't know what that is. To have people around me whom I don't even know, let alone a husband!"

"Lucia, if your father wants this, we must not fight it. You should know that he is a good person, and he wants only what is best for his children. What I can do for you is try to obtain a one-year engagement."

"One year?! That is all I have left, so little? I feel chased away!" Lucia started to cry. "Mother, do you know any more about this?"

"I know only that a messenger from Lisbon is here on behalf of the family in question. I believe this is an official request. You will meet this emissary over dinner tonight. And, my dear Lucia, we women are powerless; we must obey. You know that I also went away from my family. Otherwise, how could I have held you in my arms now?"

"You are right, mother, I will think about it."

"You must accept it, sweetheart," Doña Alba said, sighing.

"Why are you sighing? Haven't you loved our father?"

"Yes, dear, yes, but..."

"But you haven't loved him as much as you loved the one you did not marry!"

"That is not true! Hush!" said the mother with a strangled voice, "– lest somebody should hear us!"

"Tell me about it!" Lucia cornered her, as if awakened from her dreams. "If you tell me about it and prove to me the sacrifice you made for this family, I promise I shall get married!"

"This will be so much easier for you, for you are not in love with anybody."

"Were you in love?"

With a sigh, Doña Alba told her how, when she was eighteen, she fell in love with a young nobleman with whom her family did not have very good relations. They had met at the introduction ball in Lisbon. She was very excited when she saw him, and she took courage and bowed before King Filipe IV. That was a year full of joy and sorrow....

In the first half, she thought she would marry Rodrigo, but Alba's family believed him to be a traitor; they thought he was on the side of the Spanish. After Alba's father's refusal, Rodrigo left oblivious to the war against Spain. And he was not a traitor!

"And what happened?"

"He died over there. I never saw him again, except for the portrait I carry with me all the time."

8

"Mother, how you have suffered! My situation is not at all as harsh. When father comes to me, I will agree to marry someone I do not love."

"Thank you, my daughter, for being so obedient!"

"You were saying that the messenger is in our house now, and we shall meet over dinner?"

"Yes, that is true! You have to make yourself beautiful, so that he can give a pleasing report when he gets back to the capital."

"Mother, show me the portrait."

"What ...portrait? No, dear, I am afraid!"

"I'm begging you, my good, dear mother!"

With a sigh, Doña Alba took from her neck a thick chain, which held a double medallion. She opened it and showed her daughter. "This is the only picture I have of him."

"Oh, such a handsome young man! How much you must have suffered! But maybe he is still living somewhere...."

"What are you talking about, child? He can't be! That is impossible!"

"Was he also from Lisbon? Maybe he is living in seclusion, just as we are here. What is his name?"

"Lucia, don't ask me to tell you!"

"Please, I will search without anyone knowing about it! Did he have a title?"

"Yes, he was a marquis ...Rodrigo de Linares. But no more, Lucia! I can't take anymore! My heart is beating so fast, and if I close my eyes, I can see the ball, my family's refusal, his departure...."

"Forgive me, mother!"

CHAPTER 4

Dom Miguel Ribeiro attended the dinner that night and obtained the letter he wanted so much, but he was not pleased. He was confused by the silence and indifference of the beautiful Lucia. One could see in her attitude a kind of sacrifice undertaken. Doña Alba had also been very restrained; only the Count was happy.

It was clear the women were hiding something. Their continual glances at each other seemed almost like a private conversation between them. The mother's eyes seemed to say *Courage, my dear Lucia!* and on the other side, the answer was *I shall do this, it is my duty.* Then Dom Miguel thought of Dom Pedro de Cantarra... "May God forgive me, but he is not worth having a saint as his wife!" Eventually he went to bed, but he was still dissatisfied.

The Count, after striving the whole afternoon to write the letter, had waited impatiently for dinner. He was most elated when he finally handed the letter to Dom Miguel. It was as if he could already see the recipient reading it. The letter conveyed a favorable answer, for he was giving Dom Pedro his daughter's hand. He hoped that through that marriage, his business in the capital would thrive. He was much less concerned with Lucia's feelings. She was so gentle and obedient, she would comply, even though she was despondent.

He could not conceive of any different way of thinking. A refusal was completely out of the question. He would throw a fairy-tale wedding for his daughter, and she would have an opulent trousseau. Everything would be worthy of his name, prestige, and wealth. Lucia was entering a family just as noble, so his concerns were minimal. She would have children, who would take all of her time, and she wouldn't have time to get bored – quite the contrary, Lucia will get rid of her melancholia. She would change, grow up, and mature. She would become a real lady, having her residence in the capital of the country. She would receive visitors; her ballrooms would be full of people, and she would manage them quite easily with great dignity. The Count knew her husband-to-be.

10

He was a young man in high demand, as they put it, popular with the ladies. But Lucia was so kind and innocent that maybe she wouldn't even notice that. The Count, in his thinking, contradicted himself. First he saw Lucia as a lady with a large entourage; then he saw her unchanged.

When the letter was safely placed next to Dom Miguel's chest, he finally sat down at the table. The Count noticed a certain reserved attitude of his ladies, but he did not pay any attention to it, for he was used to their humors. The dishes came one after the other, to the pride of the Count who was pleased that his servants had outdone themselves. Everything had been perfect, from the meal's beginning to end. The ladies, though….

When dinner was over and everyone left to his or her own room, it was already late, and the Count, closing the door to his apartment, told himself he had sealed a good bargain. He was aware of the envoy's apprehensions, but both the ladies went to the girl's room.

"Courage, my dear! We only have to hope in God!" said Doña Alba. "There's no other way! You will have a one-year engagement and that is at least something. When you meet Dom Pedro, you will also receive your engagement ring, and then everything will be sealed. Your father will decide when we will receive the visit of the Baron's whole family. We will be so busy with the preparations! There will be so much work to do!"

"Should I dare trust and hope in God or in a miracle preventing this from happening? I shall get married without knowing real love. You had that good fortune, but what about me?"

"Keep silent, my sweetheart! What good fortune was that? He left with his pride hurt by the refusal, and his head held up to death!"

"Maybe he is not dead! Maybe he lives in Lisbon! I shall search for him! You two will meet again!"

"Lucia, hush, in the Holy Virgin's name! What are you trying to do? I've learned to repress my feelings during all these years. Sometimes, I open the medallion … and then I can be calm again!"

"Somehow I feel he is still alive! You don't have to do anything improper, only to know that he is still alive, rather than dead. Maybe he is married; maybe he hasn't forgotten you."

"Lucia, you are becoming a dreamer again. Stop thinking about impossible things! I will let you get some sleep. I wonder what that man thought of us. We barely talked to him – your father did most of the talking…."

"That is his problem, dear mother …. I don't care! Everything has been decided upon. What difference does it make if we spoke or not over the meal. Nothing changes this situation, nor the fact that I am going to

11

marry someone whom I shall see for the first time in my life at our engagement party!"

"Good night, my sweet child!"

"Good night, mother! I can hardly wait for Francisco to come home!"

In the morning, very early in the morning, actually, Dom Miguel left for Lisbon. He had a long and tiring trip ahead of him. He had obtained the desired letter, after all, so why would he care about the concerns of others? Not everybody marries for love. There are other important interests there. With that thought in his mind, he rode slowly, with no rush, to Lisbon, for the goal of the Baron had been attained.

CHAPTER 5

On Sunday morning, everyone in Santa Cruz, the small town near Coimbra, went to the church. For hundreds of years, this town held strong ties to Coimbra, was taking pride in the Monastery of the Holy Cross. Saint Teotonius had laid the first stone in its foundation. Inside, two kings were buried, namely Alfonso Henriques and Sancho I. The monastery was renovated a century before by King Manuel I, who had moved the two kings' eternal resting place somewhere else, still in the monastery, however, because of their importance.

Everyone walked together, irrespective of social rank. It was a way of showing that everyone was equal before God in His Holy Church, but especially before the Holy Inquisitional Chair.

So on their way that Sunday morning, the family of Count de Sousa y Monterro was walking to the church to hear the Holy Mass held by the monks of that monastery. They were going to meet other Christians whom they would greet solemnly, and it was as if the first day of the week made them more introverted and more concerned about their souls and the Catholic faith. No matter how faithful they were during the week – and they were, thank God for that – on Sunday, they would outdo themselves. They washed themselves and put on their best clothes, but especially they were full of piety.

Next to the place where the monastery was built, the Count's family met the family living on the domain next to them, namely the family of Count Joaquim de Luso. These families seldom visited each other, but since the two sons had studied together in the capital, rumor had it that they also cavorted together, for they were best friends. The de Luso family had two daughters besides their heir, Luis, and Lucia would meet them quite frequently. They wrote to each other, and they walked together; they also rode together on the bank of the river. They socialized, as well. There were not many noble families in the area, and they were glad for each other's company. Luis's sisters, who were nineteen and seventeen, had compassionate and submissive natures, thus perfectly matching Lucia.

13

Catarina, the elder one, had recently become engaged, and she glowed with happiness, shining just like the ring on her left hand. It was she that Lucia would have liked to question at length. Was in she in love, or was she fulfilling a duty? Lucia thought that after arriving home, she would write to her, saying that she absolutely must see her.

After ceremoniously greeting each other, the two men talked about their sons' upcoming return home. What would they do afterwards? What would their concerns be, now that school was over. The next week, two weeks at the latest, they would arrive. Everyone looked forward to their return.

Arriving at the monastery chapel, the two families separated, taking their places reserved for them for so many years. For the first time, Lucia was not attentive and did not give the responses during the Mass. Her mother drew her attention, lightly nudging her in the ribs. Lucia startled, but then went back to the questions churning in her mind: what is love like? Did she really have to get married? Was she forced to? Would she endure it? What is Dom Pedro like? Her questions remained unanswered. This was a marriage of convenience, but that convenience was not hers.

She didn't matter. For the first time, she acknowledged that that was not right, that she was a mere tool. She realized that until then, she had lived with her head in the clouds, and now reality brought her down to earth. And Mother — how could she have done that? How could she have submitted to that, how can she endure? What if that man is still alive? Lucia would search for him in that huge Lisbon, as large and forbidding as an ugly dream.

The Mass was over. Lunchtime passed by as well, during which Lucia just picked at her food. Her father talked enthusiastically about the kind of life he thought she would live in the capital, where she would get to see the king quite frequently. She would always be richly dressed; she would have a carriage, servants, an exciting life, totally different from the one she had there in Santa Cruz de Coimbra.

After the meal, she left to go to the park alone; she just wanted to go for a walk and try not to choke. How could she be snatched from her house and given away to a stranger? She was looking forward to her brother's coming home. She would talk to him, and together they would come up with a solution. Maybe he knows her husband-to-be. Maybe he knows what he is like, what character he has, what he looks like....

She wondered where the Lucia from the previous week was. Where is the girl who would settle for the trills of her canary? The girl who would frolic like a deer? She had to pray for a miracle, for soon she

14

would meet her future husband. The Holy Virgin had to give her strength. Her mother wouldn't be there by her side, either. How often would she visit her family afterwards?

She realized that her mother, during all her life as a married woman, had rarely gone to see her parents. Thus, the same fate lay ahead of her. How often would she see Francisco after that? He will get married soon, too. But he will stay here, at home. She was so profoundly tied to every single thing in Santa Cruz! She loved the river, the church, and the poor people whom she helped at times, and whom she would visit together with her mother. Heavy tears were falling down her cheeks and onto her dress.

"A miracle, God, please make a miracle! Give me a sign, help me calm down, and give me strength!"

Then she ran to the end of the park, so that nobody should see her or her weakness anymore. She would collect herself before she returned, but now she needed to cry and be alone. She stumbled and fell, and then cried even more.

Somebody handed her a flower. It was the good, old gardener.

"O, José, I am so miserable!" Lucia said, taking the flower. "They will have me marry someone I have never seen, whom I do not love either!"

"Dear young lady, do not trouble yourself! Sometimes life doesn't come out the way others want it to…."

Quietly, he took her to his simple, clean, and airy house. Lucia became calmer after being given a cup of fresh milk.

"It is going to be all right, you shall see!"

"You, José, you followed my mother from her parents' house…. You remind her of the place where she was born…."

"That is true! She was allowed to bring me with her! I know her secrets and all her tears, and I don't want her daughter to go through the same sorrow as her mother!"

"Do you know about the Marquis de Linares?"

"Yes, my girl, he was the most noble man I have ever met. He was not a traitor! He loved your mother. I used to carry their correspondence, which is why I am telling you it is not possible for two fates to be just the same. Now go, relax, and collect yourself!

"Come and see me again, I shall tell you about it, maybe, who knows?"

15

CHAPTER 6

Lucia seemed to come back to life after hearing the news one morning that Francisco was coming home. He had finished school, and he was ready for his duties as heir.

"Probably he should get married, too," Lucia thought.

Everyone was busy with preparations for the reception. The young man had announced that he would travel together with Luis de Luso, his good friend. The news pleased everyone as he would have company on his long journey. The young men were approximately the same age and got on well with each other, had always supported each other, and had spent the past years together.

Lucia did not know young Luis as no one had introduced them. After all, she was younger and hadn't been presented to society yet. She thought she had probably seen him at church, at the place of the de Luso family, but had not noticed him. She knew he went to the same school as her brother, and they were the same age, but that was all. She spent more time with Catarina and Joana.... "Happy Catarina for being engaged! I should be happy, too!"

Francisco and Luis were traveling in the de Luso family carriage, so Francisco's family immediately sent a thank-you letter to the de Luso household. In fact, according to Francisco's most recent letter, his friend agreed to pay a courtesy visit to Santa Cruz. So everything should be perfect, right on time.

They all knew that Francisco would be home that night and that Luis de Luso would not leave the carriage, hurrying to get to his home where everybody was so excited. The de Luso domain was twenty kilometers farther. In fact, the only time they left Luso was on Sunday when they went to the church in Santa Cruz. They were the only ones coming from such a distance on Sunday, reaching there by carriage. During the week, they attended the religious services at their local church, but for many years, they had gone to the church in Coimbra on Sunday – a custom that could not be changed.

Lucia was standing by the window in her room watching the road. Her parents were waiting on the ground floor in the library. Surely the carriage must be near. It was already dark. And there on the horizon, Lucia suddenly saw a dot which grew bigger and then became a carriage bestirring the dust, then leaving it behind.

"Mother, he's coming! I can see the carriage!" she shouted out the window.

The parents, with all the windows of the library open, heard her and ran outside to greet Francisco. Lucia would greet him inside; that was the rule. But sitting on the window ledge, she was also outside, waving to her brother, unseen by her parents. He saw her and waved his handkerchief back at her. A state of confusion occurred when the parents, seeing the sign, looked for their own handkerchiefs. But then the carriage was already on the gravel in front of the entrance.

Dom Felipe greeted his son and was greeted by his son's friend.

"Please thank your father, Count de Luso, for allowing Francisco to come with you."

"I shall tell him, but there is no need to concern yourself; it is a great honor for us all!"

Suddenly, from some place higher up, somebody sneezed. The two young men looked up in curiosity.

"Bless you, sister! Be careful not to catch a cold. Come down and hug me!"

"Welcome home, beloved brother! I've been up here waiting for you for a long time! I saw the carriage from a distance and sounded the alarm!"

"Thank God you did not blow the trumpet! The sneeze was enough," he laughed loudly.

During all that time, Luis was looking up to the girl's window. "What a lovely sister Francisco has! How is it I have not noticed her before?" When their eyes met, he could not stop gazing at her. Lucia bowed, confused without understanding the reason, and moved away from the window.

"Luis, this is my sister. She is as shy as any other girl … I'll see you tomorrow; how about going for a ride?"

"Yes, I'll see you in the afternoon, to go and see the surroundings, notice the changes. Now I have to go, they are waiting for me! But you are lucky, you are already home."

"So long, Luis, and thank you!"

The carriage left, and Luis waved goodbye. He looked up, but no longer saw that creature that so captivated him. "That's odd, no woman

17

has ever made my heart jump, and God knows, as Francisco is my witness, there have been enough…. That's curious. I have to think about this. I shall accept the invitation to lunch, and she will be there, too. Where have they been hiding her?"

Lucia moved away from the window, her heart almost jumping out of her chest. She contained herself and greeted her brother happily.

"Lucia, you've grown up, you are a real young lady now!"

"Engaged," Dom Felipe answered for her….

"Already? To whom?"

"Pedro de Cantarra. A wonderful deal for the wellbeing of both families."

"Who? Hmm!" Francisco almost imperceptibly changed, then quickly recovered. But Lucia saw and understood that there was something about that man, something that her brother knew.

"Mother, dear mother, you look very good! Always younger…"

"Flatterer! Give your mother a kiss!"

The evening was pleasant, but short. Francisco was tired, but asked his father to join him in the library after dinner. The ladies had gone to bed, for they were weary from the emotional day.

When both had closed the door behind them, Francisco started talking first.

"Father, why Pedro de Cantarra of all men? He is a rascal, a rogue with no honor. They say that he has a child out of wedlock, with an actress. His parents paid a great deal to keep her mouth shut! Lucia deserves a better fate!"

"There is no point in interfering with my business! He will marry Lucia and will come to his senses!"

"Pedro will never come to his senses! Lucia will die of grief. Is this what you want?"

"This marriage will be concluded, no matter what your opinion might be! It's already been decided! They will come here in two months' time, to propose to her. I'm already waiting for a positive answer regarding the visit."

"Obviously, you will do whatever you wish and have decided upon, dear father, but this is all wrong! This is a bad choice! Pedro will never change!"

"I want you to stay out of it, Francisco!" His father lifted his voice in irritation.

"I repeat, father, you will do what you please. Lucia's happiness is your decision and your responsibility. I have only warned you about him.

Let's not talk about this subject anymore. In fact, I am tired. I want to go to my room. I have been looking forward to being with you again."

"Yes, son, it has been decided upon, and you shall not change my mind. Now go and get some sleep, you are tired. Everything is set. I shall linger here a little longer. Welcome home. "

"Thank you, father, good night."

What demon, what foreboding made Lucia come out of her room and go downstairs? And listen to the dialogue between the men of the family? A tremendous pain made her stand still, and only her tears proved she was alive. When Francisco came out of the library, he saw her and understood it all. He took her in his arms and started walking up the stairs.

"Lucia, Lucia, compose yourself, sweet sister of mine! I promise you I shall do everything in my power to prevent this marriage!"

"Fate is adverse to me! My father has made a decision and I must abide by it. Francisco, what does it mean, to love? When I saw Luis de Luso, for the first time I grew unsettled. My heart started pounding as if wanting to come out of my chest. I got so upset that I almost fainted. I rubbed my temples with some water. I had to be able to celebrate your coming home."

"Lucia, would those be the first love thrills? I prefer Luis a thousand times to that rapscallion Pedro and his scandalous behavior."

"What does my future husband look like?"

"He is not ugly at all. He is rich, and he is very attractive to women. He is chased by every noble girl for his fortune and he has an infamous character. Girls from society in the capital are different; all that matters to them is money and jewels, the box at the Opera House and the carriage with the coat of arms. You are not like that. You are kind and made to love. I am afraid you will lose yourself!"

"He has a child!"

"Yes, but he doesn't care! As I can see, he wants a benign and naïve wife, willing to tolerate all his outbursts. That is why, I think, he – the Baron de Cantarra – thought of father,. He knows that father has a daughter and thinks that his son's indignities have not reached Coimbra. But you see, everybody knows about them."

"And Luis? I mean your friend?" Lucia became flustered....

"You are on the verge of loving, do not hide it from me...."

"No. Forgive me!"

"Luis too knows about Pedro's child and his outrageous behavior. Lucia, we have also done all kinds of pranks, but up to a point, to a limit."

"I understand. I must resign myself!"

"Maybe not; the engagement is not finalized yet – then there will be one more year after that. Many things can happen during that time. Now I want you to calm down. Listen to me and go to bed. Think of something nice. Love, for instance!"

"It died in the bud, Francisco, don't you see that? I am a girl from the province, I cannot cope with the two-faced society in the capital."

"We shall see about that! Now go to sleep," her brother told her, kissing her on the forehead. Lucia smiled sadly, weakly, distrustful.

The following day, the two best friends met, making a exploration of the area.

"Nothing ever changes around here," said Luis.

"That is true!"

"Francisco, I caught a glimpse of your sister last night. She is very beautiful, yet she seems delicate and melancholic. I think she is the kind of woman that any man would love and would do anything to protect her. I would like to get to know her better. I like her. I am so sick and tired of those shallow girls in the capital. She is different."

"Lucia? Are you talking about my sister?"

"Yes, I saw her last night. She is wonderful! I shall accept your father's invitation as soon as possible, to get the chance to talk to her, to listen to her."

"I would say you're in love ... you too...."

"What do you mean, me too?"

"Lucia saw you as well last night. I think she is in love for the very first time, but this is impossible love, which will be never fulfilled...."

"Why not? As far as I am concerned..."

"As far as you are concerned, nothing, Luis.... She is promised to Dom Pedro de Cantarra. Lucia will wash his dirt with her purity. My father has a deal with Pedro's father. He has all kinds of business. Lucia is the trade."

"Holy God, I am astonished!"

"So am I. I had a talk with my father last night, but in vain. She is already promised. In two months' time, he is coming here to officially propose to her. Then there will be a one-year engagement, and then Lucia will vanish like merchandise. Father has always been just and kind, but all in a peculiar form, typical of him. He thinks this is the best thing he can do for her. The marriage to this good-for-nothing man. His fantasy of life in the capital will do Lucia no good. Worst of all, she overheard my conversation with father, including the part related to that actress and her child."

"She must be devastated."

"Knowing her as I do, she will slowly die away. My father has no eyes to see that."

"I wish I could meet her! But with no servants around us. What can I do?"

"Every morning, after breakfast, Lucia rides by herself on the bank of the river. You could meet her tomorrow, and any time you want, if you are careful. I could come, too, to let you know if there is danger around or if someone may see you."

"Yes, indeed, that is a good idea…."

The two friends and accomplices said nothing more; they just rode at a slow pace, each with his own thoughts.

CHAPTER 7

Between Dom Felipe and his son, the topic of Lucia became taboo after Francisco made one more attempt to convince his father. In fact, Francisco understood that he could not move the old count out of his self-indulgent stubbornness, so unnatural for him. For certain, Francisco thought, there is something more going on than a mere financial deal or whatever the nature of that deal was. His father's perseverance seemed suspicious to him, but he could not insist upon it further, for he was not the master.

He tried to talk to his mother, but it was as if she could not hear him. She had resigned herself, too, with regard to her daughter's fate. She had one simple reaction: when Francisco told her about Pedro's child, she exclaimed: "Jesus Christ, may Holy Mary watch over her. Her fate is already sealed. Lucia is resigned to this situation, and then too, not all marriages are out of love!" Francisco tried to remind Doña Alba that Lucia was different and that she would not endure that martyrdom. His mother remained silent, her only emotion showing in the bitter tears flowing down her cheeks. Francisco, his head bent down, left his mother's room.

In the morning, Lucia ordered the equerry to saddle her dear horse. "I shall take him to Lisbon; I should get at least that, even if there are no fields there to go for a ride" Lucia thought while waiting. "There must be a park, something. The Baron is rich. This will be my only consolation. We shall both cry, and he will understand." Francisco found her waiting.

"What is my beautiful and kind sister doing?"

"I'm getting ready for a ride; I'm going to the river."

"I'm joining you, and so is Luis. He loves you, he confessed to me yesterday. I told him about Pedro, and he is horrified."

"Tell him not to love me, for it is in vain. We do not stand a chance. Even if I begged father on my knees, with tears in my eyes, I couldn't change anything. In fact, I have not even tried; it is useless. I do not want to humiliate myself for nothing. I have to preserve some dignity. I shall manage somehow to overcome all this. It sounds as if Pedro is a flirt; perhaps he will go on with this addiction, and then he will ignore me. I shall remain in my room, I shall pray and I shall read. Life will pass, hour by hour."

"Maybe. Let's go."

Side by side, the two siblings started off to the river. Luis had already arrived there and was waiting for them. He got off his horse and tied him to a willow. He was throwing stones into the water. Francisco and Lucia also got off their horses. Francisco touched his hat brim and said:

"I shall be close by, no worries."

"All right, but do not go too far," Lucia replied, gazing at him.

After Francisco vanished from sight, Luis took Lucia by the hand, and they both sat down on his large coat. He stopped throwing stones into the Mondego River. They just sat there for a long time holding hands, not uttering a word.

"Lucia, allow me to tell you that last night, when I saw you, for the first time I felt a flash in my heart. I think I love you. I feel restless, I am happy when I think of you. This is something I have never felt before."

"Luis, my good Luis, you know that by this time next year, I shall belong to another man. I felt the same thing last night. Fright made me withdraw from the window. I have never had much company here, except for your sisters on Sunday, and sometimes on short visits. I do not understand why my father would want to have me married before my debut. But I have accepted it. I shall never love my husband. I understand that this union is a matter pertaining to certain business interests, and that they have nothing to do with feelings. Pedro is a skirt chaser and I do not think I shall be able to change him. Therefore I have resigned myself to that. I shall love you eternally. I am not ashamed to admit that to you openly, because I know this love is impossible."

"Lucia, what if we eloped?"

"Don't be a child, Luis. Soon, you will love another girl, for it will be impossible to marry me."

"You can't dictate to your heart whom to love – you know that only too well, my dear."

"I know, but I accepted the marriage. Francisco tells me that mother did the same, that there is more than a year until then, that I have to be brave, and that many things may happen."

"You will not marry him, Lucia, I do not want that! I can't see you belonging to another man, while I just sit there and do nothing. Please, promise me you will think about it. They are right, it is a year and a half almost, and many things may happen in one hour, in one day, not to mention a year!"

23

"I will think about it because this is what you want, my dear Luis." Just then, they heard a slight noise.

"That is it, children," Francisco said, "someone is coming over."

The two of them stood up, trembling. Luis kissed her hands and let her go.

"I shall see you tomorrow; I shall wait for you both here every morning. I shall throw all the stones into the river."

"We will see you tomorrow," Francisco replied. "Let's go, Lucia!"

His brother lifted her up and sat her on her horse, as if she had been a flake. She was so sad, her eyes looking straight into Luis's eyes. He remained on the bank. He did not dare take a step closer. The two of them left for their home. They had already stayed too long, but no one had an objection to that, for they were together and safe.

Day after day, the three young people met by the river, where the romance grew stronger and stronger like a baby in its mother's womb. They tried making plans, but their plans would topple like fortresses with too few soldiers, left to the will of the enemy. On Sunday, they would greet each other ceremoniously, not showing they knew each other better than they should have. But they were content with that. Nobody suspected anything, and even though they could not touch each other, they could still look at each other.

They were fond of the river and the grassy riverbank. It was as if that spot belonged to them both. Francisco was their accomplice, and they could go for a walk holding hands with nothing to worry about in that respect. The weather was on their side, too, as if supporting the two hearts. In the evening back at their own homes, each brought to mind the image of the other. They would dream and forget that as time went by, the visit of the official fiancé was getting closer.

Lucia gave Luis a handkerchief, and he slept with it close to his lips all the time. He also found a hiding place to keep it. He would ardently kiss Lucia's embroidered initial "L" and the coat of arms of the de Sousa family. Nobody in his family knew anything about the handkerchief; he composed himself only too well.

It was easier for the other tormented soul, given that she had a confidant, a shoulder to cry on, without anyone suspecting anything. Everybody knew about the bond between the two siblings, so nobody paid any attention to their constant companionship; their riding together every morning was considered normal and healthy. It was even recommended by the Count, considering that in a few months' time, she would not have a place to ride anymore. There was a river in Lisbon, of course, but a lady would not ride unaccompanied, and Lucia would not have the freedom she had in the countryside, in the province.

Francisco and Lucia were living in a dream from which they didn't want to awaken. They did not think a break-up would be possible, nor the intervention of someone from outside. Francisco, lost in his thoughts more than ever, could see how the affair might get out of control when he caught Luis embracing Lucia and holding her passionately to his chest.

"Oh miracle, oh miracle," he thought, biting his lips until they bled, "it would be so much better if she belonged to Luis and not Pedro!"

CHAPTER 8

The days passed, one by one, serene and full of sunshine. At the castle, everybody was still waiting for the letter announcing the visit of the Baron de Cantarra and his entourage. The two lovers were the only ones hoping that they would never come and wanting the whole arrangement to be off.

But, unfortunately, the fateful day came when the long awaited letter arrived and was in the hands of the Count de Sousa. It announced the matchmakers. The visit was to take place in precisely one week. The Baron de Cantarra was coming with his wife and his son Pedro, together with a host of servants worthy of his rank. Everyone was caught up in the fever of the preparations. They dusted and cleaned all the rooms in the wing where the noble family lived as well as those in the servants' area. In the kitchen, cooks were planning menus; they would prepare fowl, beef, and sheep. The Count wanted to amaze the Baron with his wealth. He didn't want to appear at all beneath the Baron's level. That engagement was far too important for his business.

On Thursday, the people appointed to watch for the Baron's arrival rushed in.

"The guests are coming!"

"Marvelous!" the Count said, throwing a purse with money to them. Is everything set, madam?"

Doña Alba replied with resignation that everything was in order. It was all right for the guests to arrive now. This visit was tiring her and interrupting the rhythm of her quiet life. For some time, she had felt that her children were hiding something from her. Francisco and Lucia had always had a special relationship – they were indeed very close – but at that moment she felt that she was missing something. She trusted Francisco, and Lucia seemed to have calmed down a little, though not completely. She would definitely have a talk with her daughter after this visit was over.

The assembly of the de Cantarra family had stopped their carriages on the platform. The whole de Sousa family was standing at the front entrance, each with his or her own disposition and state of mind. The Count was happy, his wife a bit troubled, Lucia wore the mask of resignation, and Francisco stood with his fists clenched, barely containing his anxiety. The servants had opened the doors and come down the stairs. The Baron got out of the carriage first, helping his wife, and behind them, the handsome and spoiled Dom Pedro de Cantarra.

After the usual proprieties of greeting, which included questions related to the journey, health, and dust in the province, the guests went upstairs to their appointed rooms to rest and change from their traveling clothes into something more comfortable. This gives plenty of time for us to describe at ease the members of the famous de Cantarra family.

The Baron, a rather old man, was still handsome for his age, and was in a good mood almost the whole time. He loved showing his charm with clothes and jewels. There was only one thing that disturbed his peace of mind: Pedro, his only child, who, it was hoped, would come to his senses and grow wiser, thanks to his upcoming marriage and the responsibility that came with it. That was the Baron's only concern. He himself had married rather late to a lady from his society who was much younger than he. We believe she was Doña Alba's age. She was not pretty – she never had been – but she had one quality for which she was cherished. She never interfered with her husband's business; she closed her eyes to all his escapades and did not seem to pay attention to anything but her clothes. We think that since she was so tolerant, her son Pedro took after his father's habits.

But Pedro, that spoiled son, was indeed handsome – handsome and spoiled: two requisites for one to enjoy a life of wealth and pleasure. Pedro was an only child, so everything by rights belonged to him. Everyone would bow to him and try to please him. His carriage could be recognized everywhere he went, for it had the coat of arms on both doors. His servants wore the most expensive clothes. His company was coveted by everybody, but especially by mothers who had daughters to marry. Even the episode with the theatre actress, although it ended badly, was forgiven.

Pedro was a witty and quite intelligent man, but the problem was that these two characteristics did not serve any good purpose; instead, they would chafe, turning in boredom from one side to the other. His spirit suddenly awoke, as if hit by a hammer, when his father told him that he troubled his peace. He did not quite understand, and so he ran to Doña Sofia, who cleared that up for him: Lucia of Sousa y Monterro.

Everything was arranged. The engagement would take place that year, and the wedding, the next year! Pedro fell down into a chair. He had never heard of a girl by that name. Ah! Coimbra…. They had to get married – or else his father, who had paid dearly for the "disappearance" of the actress with the baby, would stop giving him money and would take the carriage away from him.

He reached his room, strangely relaxed and lucid. He had no choice but to go through with the marriage. His mother had told him that for his wedding, he would get a substantial monthly allowance and the palace near the park Vasco da Gama. So marriage… It shall be done! Thus, he arrived at the castle of de Sousa in a reasonably good mood. He was curious to see his fiancée. His mother had put in his trunk the jewels for his fiancée, plus the ring she had received from his father when they were engaged. That was a family tradition.

Thus we end the description of the de Cantarra family. We should add only that Pedro was not exactly the epitome of evil, he was just rich and reckless.

To Pedro, Lucia seemed like a prude, come down from the monastery to redeem him. He didn't think he liked her. What could he possibly see in a girl raised in the countryside and not yet introduced to society? She was only sixteen. How could his father have made that choice? His wife… He became terrified at the thought that he would see her only praying. How would he get close to her?

The dinner was lovely for those in a good mood. After dinner, Pedro went upstairs to his room and got the jewels… "Let's get this comedy done with, once and for all," he said to himself. He went back downstairs to the parlor, where he respectfully asked the Count de Sousa for his permission to marry his daughter Lucia. The Count accepted the proposal and gestured for Pedro to approach Lucia. She stood up like a coiled spring, waiting. "There is something about this girl; she is hiding something…." Pedro couldn't shake that feeling. But he knelt theatrically and gave Lucia the boxes of family jewels. Then, he put the ring on her finger… "What do you know… it fits!" he laughed. He took her hands and let them go. Then he took her by her shoulders and kissed her forehead. Pedro was shocked. "She is as cold as death!" But she did not reveal anything to explain her silence.

"Something is going on here!" Pedro thought again. The girl smiled at him shyly. She was engaged! But that troubling moment passed, and everyone began to feel comfortable. The two family patriarchs were quite pleased.

"Count, if I may, would you be so kind as to allow me to take my fiancée out for a walk? She can show me the park."

"Go, children … you go, Lucia…."

Lucia put the jewels back in the boxes and gave them to her mother, then went outside. They started walking, silent, next to each other. Pedro, confused, said finally:

"Dear Lucia, you are so quiet, and you look so miserable and distracted…"

"You are wrong, Sir!"

"And look how you talk to your husband-to-be!"

Lucia sighed, and Pedro stopped her and took her by the hands.

"You don't want to get married, do you? To a stranger with a bad name. Well, you should know that I don't want that either, but if I don't marry you, my father will cut off my money and take my carriage. We can work out some arrangement after the wedding. You don't have to belong to me! I feel you are different; you are not like the women I know. Maybe you love someone else …"

"I am grateful to you for what you have said just now. I know you have a child."

"Everybody knows it, and now so do you. Does that bother you?"

"No! Not at all! A child is a blessing. You should marry his mother, not me."

"My father paid her to go away."

"That is a shame! That child is your flesh and blood. You should look for her. That child must have everything he needs."

"You are so kind and I can see this does not bother you. You are the first sincere, straightforward woman I have talked to!"

"Shall we go back? I want to go upstairs to my room. I am tired; there have been too many emotions today."

"Lucia, is there someone you love?"

"Yes, and this is precisely why I am grateful for what you said earlier. We shall do what our parents want us to, but do not ask for more from me."

"I couldn't possibly. You are far too sensitive. I don't even know how to have a conversation with you."

"Pedro, let's agree to something. Let's not lie to each other. Let's each of us do whatever he or she wants, without hurting the other."

"Promise! This is only too fair, as far as I'm concerned. Do you like the ring?"

"Yes, it is nice, but it doesn't matter too much."

"I see…"

The two engaged young people entered the parlor in peace. They seemed to have come to an understanding.

"We were just talking about you two," the Baron said. "Lucia, you must come to Lisbon for the trousseau, and to pay some visits, and we and Pedro shall come and visit you during this year. Pedro will receive a palace where you shall live in the finest manner. You won't lack anything to make you happy."

"Thank you, father!"

The ladies asked to be excused, then went to bed. Lucia was relieved after having locked her door. She immediately took the ring off. "Never! Never!"

Pedro took Francisco aside and told him: "Do not think I am some kind of cad; I made a deal with your sister, so I won't touch her. In fact, she even confessed to me that she is in love with somebody else. She told me that I should look for my child, and make sure he has everything he needs. And she is right about that. I have to change! Lucia is a saint!"

"My sister has a noble soul, but she belongs to another man. She will not love you. Maybe she will be just your friend, nothing more, and she will help you change your character. After you get married, she will not betray you, but she will not love you, either."

"May I know – who is the man she loves?"

"Yes, it is Luis de Luso. He lives near us."

"I know the man, and he is indeed what Lucia would need. What a pity this is impossible!"

The discussion ended abruptly. Pedro bowed and went upstairs to his room.

CHAPTER 9

A few days later, the guests left to go back to Lisbon, inviting the Count's family to return their visit when they came to the de Sousa house in the capital. For Lucia, but especially for Luis, those had been days of real torture. Lucia would put the ring on her finger, and then take it off in the evening. Luis would come to the river every single morning and sit and throw stones into the water, wishing that the visit that was keeping Lucia away from him could end sooner.

When she was free again, Lucia decided not to wear the ring in front of Luis. She had to be careful, but that was what she wanted. After the de Cantarras left, they met again, and their love was even more ardent due to the waiting. When Lucia was in her lover's arms, their kisses, shy in the beginning, grew more and more passionate. They forgot that in one year's time, Lucia would leave for good. They did not want to think of that; it hurt too much. Luis held Lucia even more tightly in his arms, until the girl could hardly breathe.

One morning, Lucia told Luis about her upcoming departure to Lisbon. She had to take care of the trousseau, the invitations, and all kinds of things that she dreaded. She had to go to different parlors and meet all kinds of people who would look at her from head to toe and interpret all her words.

"And what am I going to do, Lucia? I shall wait for you to come every single day, and you won't be there."

"What about me, Luis? You have the river; everything around it speaks about our love, but I shall have to bear looking at people. I shall have to wear the ring. I shall have to make up a trousseau that I don't want. I mean, I want a trousseau, but married to you. Your kisses are burning me; I shall remember them through the whole journey. I am devastated, Luis. I feel like crying all the time. And, above it all, I shall see him, and his ostentatious wealth."

"Forgive me, Lucia! You are more miserable than I am. Forgive me, my love! You have never worn the ring in front of me, lest you should hurt me. Forgive me! While you are gone, I shall think about this; I shall make a plan. We must elope, and I shall talk to Francisco. Will you come with me? We shall elope to Spain, and we shall get married there!"

"I'll follow you anywhere, Luis; you are my only love. Until then, please wear my medallion around your neck. Inside, there is a portrait of me and a lock of my hair. I shall be close to you. You will close your eyes and you will feel my hands."

Luis took the golden chain from his neck. It had a beautiful little cross.

"You wear this, and when you look at it, I shall be there, too, next to you. My mother gave it to me a few years ago, when I turned twenty. And we shall write to each other! We shall find a way, through a secret messenger. And when you come back, everything will be all set."

"All right, my dear Luis."

Lucia, Doña Alba, and Francisco left for Lisbon. The Count did not have the necessary patience for that. He was happy, like a child with a new toy. He knew absolutely nothing about his daughter's love for their neighbor.

They arrived late at night, and the torches were burning in front of the small palace with aigrettes. The servants were waiting for them; the house was empty almost all the time. While Francisco studied at the University, he used only the library. He never took the time to go to a room upstairs. He had turned the library into a bedroom, parlor, and study, all in one. Anything to keep from going upstairs. The servants did not insist upon that. They let the young master alone. But now, it was a different story, so everything was cleaned and aired out, and the covers were all taken from the furniture. The mistresses were coming, and even Francisco had his own room all set for him.

The tailor was expecting them the next morning, so they had to go to sleep quickly. A trousseau was hard to make even for someone less prominent, not to mention for the fiancée of the most desired man in Lisbon. Everyone was curious to see Lucia, the "illusion-breaker." When she entered her room, a young girl dressed as a servant knocked at her door and, with her finger to her lips, gave Lucia a letter from Luis.

"Oh! What bliss, what a wonderful surprise!"

"Dom Luis is waiting for an answer today, so hurry, the man who will take it is waiting."

Lucia started writing. What happiness, what a delight! She thanked him with thousands of kisses. Lucia's sadness went away as her words were laid down on the pink paper. She kissed the envelope again before sealing it; she had put in it a flower from the bouquet in the vase. But the young maid had hardly left her room when Doña Alba entered.

"I have been watching you for some time now. What are you hiding from me? What was that girl doing here so late? You wrote a letter and I believe that it was not for Pedro!"

"Mother ..." Lucia said sadly.

"Lucia, do not hide this from me; no one will find out anything. I know that you and Francisco are tied by more than brotherly love. You two share a secret."

"Yes, mother! I love Luis de Luso and he loves me back. I cannot marry Pedro! I do not love him, and he knows it. He knows that I love Luis. I advised him to look after his child."

"Lucia, my dear, where is this going to take you? I suspected something, but I couldn't find out anything. Francisco is a very good confidant. What are you going to do?"

"We shall wait until next year, and, when the time is right, we shall elope!"

"Dear, you shall dishonor your father!"

"Mother, I am in love. I cannot give in as you did. I cannot live a miserable life, and I cannot endure all of this. I shall resist! I don't understand how you could live for so long next to a man whom you don't love, always thinking of the other man?"

"Keep silent, Lucia, do not talk about the dead!"

"How do you know that he's dead? You have gone only as far as Coimbra! Your universe! You've seen your parents so seldom, dear mother! I cannot live like that; I'd rather die! I promise you I shall conduct myself as honorably as possible during this time, but I beseech you, mother, do not ask for more from me – and keep my secret!"

"What are you asking from me, Lucia?"

"To close your eyes! To let me love. To love! To fight! To elope, if need be. To help me!"

"I cannot let you elope!"

"If you love me, you will!"

"You've changed, Lucia! Love has changed you! You are stronger than I am. I was a coward."

"Mother, please give me the medallion of Marquis de Linares."

"What do you need it for?"

"I want to have it for a few days. I have a plan and I want to find out if the marquis is dead or alive. Please give it to me!"

Doña Alba gave in to her daughter, handing her the medallion. She had never been apart from it.

"Here it is, but only for a few days! I am going to bed, my daughter. May God watch over you!"

"Good night, mother!"

The next day, at the tailor's, everything was a tiresome burden. Lucia did exactly as she was told, in order to take her measurements. She was not one of those happy brides, and the tailor could sense that. Everyone in the capital had their wedding dresses made by her, so she had learned to sense people like a bloodhound... "This marriage is forced, but I wonder why?" Lady Gloria, the tailor, thought to herself, continuing to study Lucia. "She is beautiful, but miserable, unhappy ... She is so young, nobody in the capital knows her." Then Lucia, as if awakened from a deep sleep, asked Lady Gloria something that made her mother cry out.

"Lady Gloria, many people come to you, so I would like to ask you a question, if you don't mind...."

"Of course, my dear. How can I help you?"

"A long time ago, more than a quarter of a century ago, I believe, there was a Marquis de Linares, ... Rodrigo de Linares, to be more precise. I would be curious to find out if he is still alive ...."

"If you are speaking about the widower Marquis Rodrigo de Linares, who fought in Spain and came back in one piece, yes, I can certify that he is alive. He is about fifty years old, but since his wife passed away, he's been living alone and secluded. We see him only on Sunday at the church; except for that, he lives in the small family palace, solitary like a hermit. Rumor has it that he is grieving not over his late wife, but over an old love. But who can know that for sure?"

"May I have his address, please?"

"Yes, why not? It is no secret! But he will not see you, I am sure."

Lady Gloria wrote the address on a slip of paper, not suspecting what she had just wrought in the soul of Doña Alba, who could barely contain herself during the trying on of clothes and everything else related to a full and complete trousseau. Only when they were in the carriage did she ask Lucia what she planned to do.

"I told you he is alive! Don't worry, I will do no harm. Each of us has a secret to keep. I have to keep yours, and you have to keep mine. Let's not talk about this anymore. I am hungry, I am bored with this Lady Gloria, and I am so tired. I think you are tired, too."

The next morning, Lucia got dressed to go out. Over her hat, she put a thick veil which hung to her waist. She asked for the carriage, indicating the address of the marquis, where she wanted to go. She took the medallion with her and left. In front of the small palace, she got out of the carriage and knocked firmly at the door. Shortly, an old man came out.

Amazed by whom he saw standing in front of him, he told her that the marquis did not see anyone; he is not available for anybody, ever.

"If you could, please just tell me if he is home," Lucia insisted.

"He is home, but he does not see anybody, as I just had the honor of telling you."

"He will see me. Could you please be so kind as to personally give him this case? I'll wait outside for his answer."

The old man took the case, shrugged his shoulders, and promised her that he would not keep her waiting long. But he noticed something – the aigrettes on the carriage doors – and congratulated himself for his small remnant of perspicacity. He turned pale and ran, if an old man can do that, closing the door.

"Dom Rodrigo, Dom Rodrigo, come quickly!"

"For what cause, Santiago, my good man, are you disturbing me?"

"Look!" Santiago opened up the medallion in front of the marquis. "This is from Doña Alba," he added.

"Where did you get this?"

"From there…," and Santiago took the marquis to the window where he could see the carriage.

"That is the coat of arms of the de Sousa y Monterro family."

"Outside, there is a lady wearing a thick veil over her face. She is waiting for an answer."

"Well, go, run and bring her here!"

"Right away, I'm flying!" And the old man ran as if he had been twenty, simultaneously with the marquis's thoughts.

"Please, come in, you are most welcome! We must get the carriage inside the yard, for it is safer this way."

"Yes, indeed."

Lucia entered a simple, yet beautifully furnished room, with the usual accoutrements of a fashionable nobleman. Time stood still around 1625, as far as the decor was concerned. She saw a tall, handsome man, who had her medallion in his hand. The marquis came towards her.

"Who are you?"

"A miserable soul," Lucia said, lifting up her veil. "I am Lucia de Sousa y Monterro. I am Alba's daughter."

"Holy God, you look so much like her! But why miserable?"

"Because destiny repeats itself. I am forced into a marriage to Baron Pedro de Cantarra, while I am in love with somebody else. Mother has never loved my father; she has always loved you, all her life. She has worn this medallion at her neck day and night, like a precious treasure.

Only yesterday did I learn that you are still alive, and I took her home closer to fainting than standing."

"Is Doña Alba in Lisbon?"

"Yes, we are here for the trousseau of this unhappy marriage."

The marquis took a seat; that was all too much for him.

"Would I be asking too much if I wanted to see her? I haven't loved anyone else, either. My wife was interested only in material things. I have a son, but he is married and he respects my seclusion. We see each other a few times a year. He lives in Porto."

"So mother loves you, and her feelings are shared, as I can see."

"Come in, Santiago; do not stand there in the door. You heard that, Alba loves me! But you, my girl, you must be rescued. The Baron's son does not have a very good reputation."

"No, he doesn't, that is true, but we have an understanding. I confessed to him that I am in love with another man, and that I know about his child. I do hope for clemency on both sides."

"Why did you come to see me?"

"I wanted to see the marks on a man's face left by unfulfilled love. I wanted to see what I shall not have to bear."

"What do you mean?"

"I cannot picture myself married to some man other than the one I love. Do you see the chain at my neck? I have it from him. I gave him one of mine as well."

"I also have something from your mother... this ring that I am wearing at my neck. I want you to give it to her, and please tell her that I am begging her on my knees to allow me to meet her – or at least consider that. I have never loved anyone else."

Lucia took the ring.

"I have to go now. I will come back, and maybe I will bring you a favorable answer, maybe not. But you will have an answer from me."

"Thank you and have courage! Fate is fate! I think I would have liked to have a daughter like you. You have shown much strength."

During Lucia's visit at the Marquis de Linares's, Doña Alba paced miles and miles across the reception parlor. She had suspected this in her soul, but she tried to refuse those thoughts; she supposed she must be dreaming. Her Rodrigo, alive! Her daughter was with him! She was so distraught that she didn't even realize Lucia had entered the room.

"Lucia, my daughter, where were you? Did you go to see... him?"

"Yes, and look what I've brought you! Your ring! He has the medallion. He loves you! And there is an old man, Santiago, who seems to be his confidant."

"I remember Santiago. My ring! My God, the chiding I got from mother for supposedly losing it! The ring got to Spain and stayed by his heart!"

"He is asking you, on his knees, to agree to see him. I must give him an answer, affirmative or not, tomorrow morning. I like the marquis; he is still handsome and seems to be so kind. I believe he has suffered a great deal. He's living like a monk; he has a son who lives with his family in Porto. They seldom visit each other. You have the whole night to sleep on it. Now if you will please excuse me, I have something to do," Lucia said and went out of the room.

Doña Alba closed her eyes, twisting and turning the ring. In a flash, she saw her whole life before her eyes, a serene and sterile life next to a man whom she had never loved and who was not at all interested in her feelings.

"Yes, I shall go to see him. I don't need a night to sleep on it, to make this decision! I deserve, if not a chance, at least a meeting!"

The next morning, Lucia took the affirmative answer to Marquis de Linares. The latter kissed her hands and thanked her. That very evening, he would see Alba, after such a long, long time. It was as if he had started living a new life. Santiago looked for some long-forgotten attire to put on, for himself, and he couldn't wait to meet her. Doña Alba, on the other hand, was so dazed that she needed three hours to get ready. She was to go there alone. Lucia refused, saying there was nothing for her to do there. And so, destiny seemed to have allowed the two lovers to be forgiven.

The two realized, without saying many words, that nothing had changed between them. Their love was the same, perhaps even stronger than before, since it was so unexpectedly found again. Through tears, they each told their stories, the double life each had had to live. But that didn't matter anymore; they decided not to be separated again, to communicate in one way or another, to see each other again, no matter how unlikely that might be, but definitely to meet again.

Lucia was envied in every parlor she visited, out of both curiosity and sheer astonishment. Everyone saw her as an innocent, sacrificed to the honor of young Cantarra. Lucia didn't care; she would just go there sometimes, to pass the time, to leave from Santa Cruz of Coimbra.

With Pedro, she kept her promise of coping with the society – the engagement, to be more precise – and she wasn't disappointed by him, either. They got on well with each other, like two good friends sharing the same goal. The trousseau was to be ready in a few weeks, and would be delivered to the house of the Count in Lisbon, to Lucia's joy.

With everything all set, the two women prepared to go, one happy in a certain way, and the other regaining her lost happiness, waiting for letters to the gardener José's address. Of course, they had to tell him the story of finding Rodrigo. They arrived home well and safely, cheerful and with no concern. The Count thought they must have had a successful visit in the capital, since they were in such a good mood after such a tiring journey. He was as blind as a new-born kitten.

CHAPTER 10

Each of the two women was happy for her own reasons. Lucia was caught in her longing for Luis, and Doña Alba was still under the influence of her own miracle. Lucia met her lover by the river as usual. She confessed to him that she would never marry Pedro. For her, life in the capital had been sheer torture; she had had to observe a formal protocol, to smile always, even if her soul was burning.

She preferred the countryside where she could run with no fear, where she didn't have to bow so much. Lucia confessed to her beloved Luis that her mother knew about their love and had promised to keep their secret. She also told him how Francisco had tried to convince Pedro to break the engagement for some reason conceived at random, but the latter refused. His own wellbeing was also at stake. He did not believe that that was something that he should do. He had promised Lucia that he would not touch her, and he thought that was enough. She was free to love whomever she pleased, but in ten months, she would be his wife, the young Baroness de Cantarra.

"That means that our only hope is to run away," said Luis.

"My mother opposes this whole thing; she will prevent us from leaving. Perhaps she will not even let me come and see you again, which would kill me. She considers that our love will have to end next year when I go away. Until then, it is like a balm, which she refuses to see. My father doesn't know anything; he is happy with his own business."

"Then what is to be done?"

"I don't really know right now. What I do know is that I will never be Pedro's. I'd rather be dead!"

"Lucia, you've seen how the weather is changing; soon, it will be cold."

"There is no problem; I have a shelter. The gardener's house. He knows about us, and his lips are sealed. You are right. We should meet there from now on. You know that the park has a hidden entrance. I will tell José to leave it open. He will be happy to do that for me. In fact, he

39

will be busy with the gardening, just as he is every fall. It will be like a house of our own. Or he may sleep in the castle; there are so many possibilities ..."

"You have thought of everything, my sweetheart!"

"Do not worry, no one will find out about it. The gardener is also mother's confidant. He is her old servant who followed her here when she got married. They share many secrets. You can come there starting tomorrow. I will tell José."

"I love you so much, Lucia! I cannot stand the thought of not seeing you. I'd rather..."

"Keep that last thought as an ultimate tragic and fateful solution, Luis. Do not say it out loud. We must part now. I will be waiting for you in the cottage I told you about. I'm going to tell José."

They kissed for a long time and then parted after the young count helped Lucia mount her horse. José did not object – on the contrary, he promised to provide a fire and warm milk every day. They could stay there as long as they wanted.

On one of those days spent in the gardener's house, Doña Alba caught them for the first time. She came to bring a letter for Rodrigo. Luis was a bit fearful at first, but Doña Alba said he was welcome.

"I fully understand you, you are like a son to me! Once I went through what you are going through now, but I was very weak and I lost my love. I have found him again with the help of this angel right here, and I shall fight for him, even if years have gone by. José knows all about it – that is why I brought him with me from my parents' home. I cried for so long in this house, until recently when I found my love again, but with no fear." Doña Alba sighed, then spoke again.

"I don't know what you will do, my dear children. Francisco and I had a talk about this, but I cannot think of anything. Moreover, time passes by so quickly! Elope where? Live like exiles? We must think about this! Next month, the trousseau will arrive here, not in Lisbon. It is better this way."

"I do not wish to see it," Lucia declared. "Lock it in a room we never use!"

Doña Alba sighed again. "You're not wearing the ring!"

"Yes, it is true; it burns me! But I'm wearing something else at my neck. This chain, which is very dear to me!"

"I understand, children! Luis, your parents, they do not suspect anything?"

"No, they do not. They are busy with Catarina's wedding, and also, they know I come to see Francisco. His friendship is accepted, and it brings them great joy. There's not much trouble you can get into in the countryside when you have a good neighbor."

"Yes, that is true, an old ally and an old confidant…. I will leave now, my dears. Lucia, please do not be late; your father doesn't know anything about this, but you'd better not raise any suspicions in him. I really don't know how this story will end!"

Winter sped past, and the two lovers still had not gathered the courage to make a plan. They saw each other less frequently, and when they could not meet, they would leave their letters at the gardener's cottage. Lucia's wedding was to take place in August, and they had almost six more months until then. It was very hard for them when they recalled that deadline, but once spring came, their hopes were rekindled. They didn't go to the river so often anymore, as it was more convenient for them to meet in the small house in the park. The gardener stayed busy, so everything was theirs.

Until this spring, their last spring together, their love had remained constant and chaste. They held each other and kissed, but they had never gone further. Luis desired her fervently, but he did not push Lucia. "When she is ready," he thought. On the other hand, Lucia wanted Luis passionately, but she was waiting for the right moment. And she could not imagine how and where that would be possible.

Then one day, José told them that he had to leave for three days to get some flowers seeds. He said that he would leave his house for them to use, giving them the keys. It seemed fate had smiled on the lovers, as if their happiness, which should have covered a whole lifetime, had been concentrated into only a few months. With José gone, they could be together, next to each other like husband and wife. Lucia, trembling all over, with the keys in her hand, asked her lover if he would come that night, if he would be able to slip all that way without being caught.

"I will be here, Lucia, three nights and three days!"

"Only the nights, Luis, we cannot disappear like this completely!"

"I love you, Lucia, and I want you completely, wholly, I want you to be mine. Is that possible? Is this something you want, too?"

"Yes, I want you to be mine. I will be waiting for you tonight in the cottage."

"I shall be there, do not worry!"

Three nights … during which Luis faced all kinds of obstacles and emotions, to get to the gardener's cottage. But those were three nights that, afterwards, seemed surreal to him – as if they had not really occurred. Lucia was so soft and beautiful, and she gave herself to him so naturally, as if it had been the most normal thing to do, wonderfully and angelically

41

tender. She seemed to have changed, to have become quieter, as if dreaming.

"Luis, what are we going to do? I cannot belong to some other man. What shall we do three months from now?"

"We shall be together, Lucia, I can feel it."

Lucia, sighing, answered with a smile: "How is it you feel that, my husband?"

The two lovers could see nothing but themselves. The family of Count de Sousa had already sent the wedding invitations to everyone they knew as well as anyone else worthy to receive such an invitation.

"Look at these invitations, my dear! These are quite marvelous little jewels! And look what a beautiful trousseau you have! You are content, aren't you, Lucia?"

"Yes, father, I am," she said, her thoughts elsewhere. Her mother tried to bring her down to earth, but Lucia was living in her own world.

Francisco personally delivered an invitation to the family of Count de Luso. Everyone was thrilled to be invited to such a wedding. Even Catarina, newly married herself, was looking forward to the event and to comparing it to her own wedding. But she liked Lucia, and she understood that this one would be more pompous. A wedding in the capital is different from a wedding in the countryside. Lucia was her friend until she married.

Lucia became more and more closed within herself. She loved Luis as much as ever, but it seemed she was hiding something else. There was only one more month before the wedding, of which the last week was to be spent in the capital, where she had not been since choosing her trousseau. But Pedro came to Santa Cruz instead, and he seemed to keep his promise. He did not even object to Lucia not wearing his ring. That had already been settled.

Then one day, as Lucia was walking with Luis and Francisco, she told them why she had been living in a parallel world.

"I am going to have a child! You son is right here in my womb. This is a marvelous happiness, which only a mother can feel!" The two men were stunned. Luis spoke first:

"What a joy... a son?"

"But what are you going to do?" That was reason talking, the reason embodied by Francisco, obviously. "There is less than a month before the wedding!"

"We shall die together, Francisco, death shall keep us united! There is no other solution, and you must respect our wishes if you truly love me. I do not want anyone to know about this. If life will not accept our happiness, death certainly will. I have tried to talk to Pedro about it, but he insists upon moving on with this miserable marriage. I have no choice."

"Luis, do you agree?"

"Yes, wholeheartedly!"

"My beloved ones, but this is a mortal sin!"

"Francisco," Luis spoke, "Lucia is right. There is no other way for us. You must promise that you will keep silent about this if you love us." Francisco, pale as death, whispered:

"Shall I pretend for a whole month?"

"You have no choice. The decision is ours. The baby is ours. The love is ours. Promise us!" Francisco insisted.

"Oh, Lord, what a tragedy! And when are you going to do this?"

"Quite soon, but obviously we shall let you know before it happens. We shall leave only a few goodbye letters."

"This is so painful! What shall I do after that? How will I live with this secret?"

"This is not your choice, my brother," Lucia told him kindly. "This is what we must do. It is our choice, each of us with our own lives."

"I could prevent you from doing this. I could shout it out tonight in the parlor…"

"You will not do it!" Lucia said, shaking him. You will not give me to that man, while I carry some other man's baby in my womb. Promise me!" Francisco, with his head in his hands, started running home, forgetting his horse.

"Poor man, I shall take his horse home. That was a shock to him…."

"For me, too, but I want to have you forever, you and our child. I did not think you could make such a decision."

"I love you, Luis! I can make such decisions. But let's think of a plan. No one must suspect any of this. Think about it, we have so little time left. We must have no regrets."

"My dear Lucia, how harsh life is for us!"

"Do not perceive it as such! The three of us will be leaving this world, so you should be happy!"

"I am!" Luis knelt down, and took Lucia's womb in his hands, kissing it.

One could not describe that picture full of such love and sorrow. Perhaps a skillful painter could have captured the scene. But there was none around, so the image remained eternal, for just the two of them. A memory that they would keep and that belonged only to them.

Every night, in his bed, Luis thought about how they should die. Lucia thought more about her poor, unborn baby. She caressed her womb, and bitter tears slid down her cheeks. Luis realized in astonishment, "I shall be a father in another world!" Then he thought of a way that would be less painful. He knew a medicine man who lived in one of the forests in the de Luso domain. He would ask him to give them some herbs, something to make them dizzy so they would not feel anything when they jumped into the Mondego river.

"Yes, this is it. Lucia must not suffer. In due time, we shall both write goodbye letters, so that we will not have to think about that in our last moments. We shall come together one more time, and then we shall drink the poison. We shall throw ourselves from the bridge and that will be the end. No suffering. I shall tell Lucia about this, and we shall die on Whit Sunday."

The next day, he told Lucia his plan. She agreed, and she was not afraid. She would be together with her beloved one. Whit Sunday also seemed to her to be a good time; there was so little time until then. No member of the two families suspected anything. Francisco was the only one who knew, and he was beside himself. He had changed completely. He was distracted, he wouldn't eat, he would ride his horse until it nearly died from exhaustion – as well as himself – and above it all, Lucia was encouraging him! Shortly before Whit Sunday, one week before they would leave for Lisbon, the two young people finished writing their goodbye letters. In fact, Luis had only one such letter to write, while Lucia wrote three. She wrote to her mother, to her brother, and to Pedro.

They waited for night to settle in, in order to disappear forever. Luis had felt several times in his pocket where he had the powders. They were there, waiting. After dinner, each withdrew to their own rooms. Lucia laid the jewels from Pedro, as well as the letters, on the bed, still neatly made from that morning. She also cut a lock of hair, which she put into the envelope for her brother. Luis wrote his last lines on his portico. He waited for the silence of night to settle in, then went to meet Lucia.

Almost running, they reached the river at the same time.

"Sweetheart, have you changed your mind?"

"No, my love. Have you?"

"No, I'll be with you until I die!" They made love passionately one last time, and then serenely, hand in hand, they gazed at the river.

"This will be our home from now on!"

"Have you brought the powders?" Lucia asked him.

"Yes, I have them right here. Shall we take them?"

"Yes, both at the same time. Let us leave this world at the same moment. Luis, kiss your wife and child!"

Luis kissed her, pressing her lips to his until they bled. He kissed her waist, which was a bit more rounded, a sign that there was a life throbbing inside her.

"My beloved son, forgive your mother and forgive your father for this!"

They swallowed the powders, which tasted brackish. At once, a powerful heat and dizziness seized them. They held hands and ran to the river. They jumped with no regrets.

Beyond this life, there was another life, which Luis and Lucia entered together, happily, with their child. They held hands, running on the green lawns, where all the creatures were talking among themselves, bidding them welcome. That was a new world with no sorrow and no pain, a world full of peace where they could feel nothing but love. They completely forgot their past, and they looked toward their future, full of confidence.

So yes, there is a new life, from where happiness smiles at every turn, eternity at its very center, and Lucia is living fully next to Luis and their baby.

CHAPTER 11

The peace of the night remained undisturbed by the fateful act of the two lovers. They held onto their resolve to the end. No one saw them, and life on earth went on without a care. The sun rose to herald a pristine, new summer day when the Whit Sunday observances would go on as usual. Or would they?

In the houses of the two families, everything was coming awake; some servants were preparing the table; others were looking after the animals while still others picked big bunches of flowers to adorn the parlors of the nobles living there. The families noticed that Luis and Lucia were not there. Luis's parents, accustomed to their son's habits, did not pay any special attention to his absence.

"He will come down eventually; maybe he came home late last night. Maybe Francisco kept him longer," each was thinking in his or her own way.

If only we could say the same thing about the events in the castle of Count de Sousa y Monterro! But that was not the case. Seeing that Lucia had not come down, Francisco dropped his fork and his face suddenly changed. He stood up abruptly, jolting the table and turning over dishes.

"Oh, Lord, no! Lucia, no!" In one second, he ran upstairs.

Doña Alba understood and rose hastily. The Count, oblivious to their fears, did not understand why they could not have breakfast in peace, when a cry of anguish and a woman's wailing made him get up from the table as well and run up the stairs. At the door, which had been slammed against the wall, the Count witnessed a heart-breaking scene. Francisco and Alba were each reading the goodbye letters, almost without breathing. Doña Alba clutched at her chest.

"My daughter's drowned! Lucia, my darling, you could not take it anymore!"

"How did she drown?" The Count asked, grabbing the other letter. "This one is for Pedro!"

46

Just then, a servant came upstairs with a shepherd who had found a scarf by the river.

"It is Lucia's! Francisco, she jumped into the water with her lover and their unborn baby!" Doña Alba grasped the truth. "We must go find them. Lucia would want us to bury them together."

"Her lover? Her child?" The Count was shouting, on the verge of apoplexy.

"Yes, my husband," Doña Alba's spoke more quietly. "Lucia was in love with Luis de Luso, and Pedro knew about that. He had promised not to touch her after their marriage. But you, Count, you are concerned only with your own interests." Her voice rose. "You don't look at anyone, and you don't listen to anyone. Francisco came to you and asked you to break the engagement, do you remember? But no, you were stubborn! Lucia did not want to upset you or to stir you from your dreams full of business! You are to blame for this!"

For the first time, Doña Alba stood up to her husband, who collapsed into an armchair. Nobody paid any further attention to him. Francisco immediately ordered a servant to go quickly to the house of the de Luso family. He was certain they knew nothing of this.

"Tell them to come here as soon as possible. We shall offer them money to compensate their honor. I shall talk to the bishop and ask him to issue a marriage certificate with an earlier date. Lucia was a saint, and Luis was my friend! Quickly, I want someone to go to Lisbon, and take these jewels and the letter for Pedro."

Francisco's orders were immediately obeyed. Francisco then went to the shepherd.

"Do you know the place? Please gather some people to go and search for them! Make sure they are good swimmers!"

"Yes, master. Come with me! We shall find them. We knew them both."

"Then, let's go," Francisco said. "Mother, please be strong! Please send someone to the Bishop, to ask him to agree to see me. And you, father, get a substantial purse of money together for the marriage of Lucia to Luis. She already has the trousseau."

It was as if his father had just awakened. Holding his hand against his chest, without uttering a word, he went to his study to count the money. There was no letter for him. He understood that he was to blame for everything. All he could do now was to restore Lucia's honor and then die. He had made a mistake. Lucia didn't tell him goodbye. So he had to follow her.

The whole village was talking about the terrible occurrence. All of the men had gone to the river to look for the two. The Mondego was calm, flowing slowly this day. The men searched, hoping they would find them. Their search started where the shepherd had found Lucia's scarf. One could still see their footprints on the riverbank. A bit downstream, a dog started barking, and then whining and howling. It had found something. Everyone ran in that direction. Francisco, completely distraught, started crying: "Lucia! Luis!"

People suddenly stopped near the dog. By an inlet, the two motionless bodies were caught between the branches of a fallen tree; a willow had halted their journey down the river. Lucia lay near her husband – together in death as in life.

"Lucia, Luis!" Francisco cried, starting to jump after them. The shepherds caught him.

"Hold him, lads! Let him calm down!"

Francisco wept unabashedly in the arms of two shepherds who after a moment released their hold, seeing him now more in control.

"Weep no more, master," they tried to comfort Francisco. "This was their fate. They are still together!"

"And what am I going to do now?"

"You shall live, to pray for them! They died on Whit Sunday. A Holy Day!"

Lucia and Luis were pulled onto the bank and wrapped in white bed sheets. The peasants brought a carriage, where both bodies were laid.

"Shall we take them both to the de Sousa castle, master?"

"Yes! They shall be together!"

The procession then began to move. Francisco walked behind the carriage, accompanied by the two lads holding him. In the meantime, the de Luso family arrived at the castle, irrational with sorrow, having the letter with them. They entered without ceremony and found the count and countess hysterical and inconsolable.

"They went to bring them from the river," Count de Sousa said without further comment. "I have here a great deal of money; I shall go to see the Bishop and offer him a price. I will ask him to give us a marriage certificate for the two of them. The Bishop has agreed to see me. That is all I can do. I am to blame for everything! I shall die soon!"

The de Luso family sat down without uttering a word. What difference did that gesture make? The count's offer was small consolation, for there was no turning back. There was also no point in screaming and shouting reproaches. The two families had always mutually understood and respected each other, and that was how they should act now when faced with pain.

The procession approached the door. The tragedy of those moments was unimaginable. Francisco had almost lost his mind and was supported by the two young shepherds; behind him was the carriage with the two bed sheets enshrouding the bodies. The parents stood in front of the platform, biting their hands out of sorrow.

"Francisco…" Count de Sousa slurred.

"Father… have you got an answer?"

"Yes, the Bishop will see us tonight. I am coming with you. Everything shall be done as you say. They shall be buried together in the de Luso family crypt. Luis's parents have already accepted this marriage agreement."

"Thank you!" Francisco addressed the Luso family.

"Don't thank us, we are also to blame. We did not know anything about their affair. They hid it all so well that there isn't much we can do, we who are still alive."

There is no point in describing further the sorrow and pain of the two families; it is understood. The Holy See consented to the marriage, and thus the honor of the two young people was restored. Thus, Lucia became Countess de Luso.

On the day of the burial, the whole populace of Luso was there, out in the street and at the cemetery. They did not dare intrude upon that profound sorrow. The family crypt was waiting for the two of them – in fact, three of them – for their eternal sleep. The ceremony was beautiful, solemn, and full of memories. One could hear murmurs, sighs, and barely contained bursts of crying from everywhere.

The most inconsolable of them all was Lucia's father. In the past few days, his chest pains had increased. He wouldn't live much longer. He could feel that. The guilt he felt for not having truly known his children was morbid. And there was something else that drove him wild: the silent reproaches of his wife. She spoke only through her eyes, and they were shouting, howling like the dog that had found the spot where the two bodies came to rest.

And Lucia, so beautiful in her wedding dress, looked as if she were sleeping. That had been her wedding. A miracle had happened, for they were not swollen by the water, but remained just as they were before, maybe due to the willow.

There was only one man who managed to slip in beside the grave. The medicine man. He started shouting:

"Curse! Curse! Be cursed, Luis, for lying to me! What did you need that powder for? To cross to the other world? You wanted to cross the river of eternity together with your lover? I hereby curse you, for the next two hundred years, to find your mate only on a Whit Sunday! One week each year!" The mourners, frightened by his wild outburst, entered the cemetery and chased him away, throwing stones at him. But the medicine man shouted as he ran, "So be it! For two hundred years!"

People who were gathered around the family burial chamber began to wail. Suddenly, Count de Sousa took a few steps, then fell facedown, gasping: "Lucia, forgive me, I'm coming to join you!" People started shouting: "A doctor! Get a doctor!" But it was too late. Francisco turned his father over, his face upward. He wasn't breathing, and all the shaking was in vain. A doctor nearby only confirmed what everyone could see. The Count was dead. Doña Alba was carried on the arms of the mourners to the carriage. The doctor was of great help to her, and shortly, she came back to her senses.

"Francisco, you must be strong for all of us! Now you are Count de Sousa y Monterro!"

"I know, mother. No pain will hold me down! And I don't believe in the curse of that man. Powders, what powders did Luis and Lucia take before? But what difference does it make? Now we have to take father home."

Count de Luso approached Francisco and Doña Alba.

"Come to our house first. We will make arrangements for the Count. You calm down a bit, and then we can leave for Santa Cruz. We are family now. We shall not leave you in these hard times."

"I am grateful to you," Francisco said, smiling.

"And I have gained a new brother," Juana said. It was as if Francisco had just discovered Juana. Her presence quieted and soothed him.

"You are right, Juana. Let's all go to the de Luso castle."

They did not linger long, only the time needed to get control of themselves and be able to carry the burden further on. Then they all went to Santa Cruz, leaving the de Luso castle in the care of the servants for a few days. Lady Luso took care of Doña Alba as if she had been her mother. Juana took care of Francisco.

"Thank you, Juana, I really needed someone in these moments – in fact, I need you, that's what I think."

Juana blushed, but did not withdraw her hands from Francisco's.

Count de Sousa, a good man, but also the greatest dreamer in the family and at the same time the most inflexible, was buried. After the guests left, the castle seemed empty to the two of them. Doña Alba was spinning the threads of her life and could not find much joy. Francisco was still young, but what about her? How could she start all over again? What could she do? She decided to go to the gardener's house; maybe there would be a letter waiting for her there.

"José, my friend, are you there?"

"Yes, mistress, and I have something for you!"

"From the Marquis? A letter! Please give it to me!"

"Here it is!"

Doña Alba read the letter. People in the capital had heard the news. They were all shocked. "The marquis is asking for permission to come and see me," Alba told José, "but I am in mourning!" This dilemma tormented her.

"Tell him that I make the house available. No one will know about it."

"Then this is what I shall do. Are you sure this is all right?"

"I think that you are getting a second chance," José replied. "Do not let it go."

"You are right. I shall write to him, and then I shall tell Francisco about it."

"Very well…"

In Lisbon, Pedro's reaction upon receiving the jewels and the letter was to become troubled. He realized how strong Lucia was in her love, while he, although he had a child, did not dare to confront his father. He remembered Lucia's words: Do not let your child grow up without a father, and your wife, live without a husband.

Holding Lucia's letter in his hand, he entered his father's study. Pedro told him that he would go search for his child and that he would give up his whole fortune for the sake of the woman who made him a father. The Baron became alarmed, and under the influence of the news from Coimbra, he relented. Pedro was his only son. He could not bear to lose him. Pedro kissed his father's hand and ran out. He took the carriage by himself, for he had no time to wait for a servant, and sped away. He arrived at his sweetheart's door out of breath.

"Maria! Maria!" She opened the door, frightened.

"Pedro, my love, you have come at last!"

"An angel sent me. She opened my eyes!"

"Lucia, wasn't it?"

"Yes. I have spoken with father. We shall get married, and we shall be together. I have a child! I shall accept my responsibilities – and I do love you! We shall be married as soon as possible, even tomorrow, and I don't care what the world may say!

"Neither do I!"

"Then get ready. We are going home. Some servants will come to pick up your things."

Their marriage took place one week later in the family chapel. There were no guests and no glamor. The child, having then a father and mother, was acknowledged as heir to the Baron de Cantarra, and they were all living in the palace originally meant for Lucia and Pedro. Where else?

We cannot conclude this chapter without describing the goodbye letters of the two lovers. Our story will continue in other chapters, but it is only fair that this chapter embrace the final contemplations of the two young people before they reached the riverbank. Lucia left three letters behind: for her mother, her brother, and her fiancé Pedro, while Luis left only one single letter. Here is the letter Lucia wrote to her mother:

"Dear mother, I had no choice. I had to make this ultimate decision. I love Luis very much, and I couldn't possibly leave him for Pedro. Then I must also tell you: I am expecting a baby by Luis. Do you recall our meetings in José's cottage? He left us the keys for a few nights, when he went to get those special seeds. Yes, I did love completely, and afterwards I couldn't possibly consider being another man's wife. This is the final and ultimate solution. I do not think I could endure what you carried for so long on your shoulders. I am glad for you and the Marquis de Linares. This is a second chance for you two. I am sure that sooner or later, you will be together. Goodbye, my dear mother, you must live and be happy for me. Farewell! I have two more letters to write, the first I wrote was for you. Don't be sad!"

To her brother:

"I dearly recall the almost maternal care you had for me not only while I was a child, but also when I grew up. Before making this decision and choosing this last gesture, I tried to picture Pedro as my husband. What I could never picture was Pedro as the father of Luis's child. Lisbon and its parlors are not for me. I was raised freely, with little of such propriety. I like it in the countryside, I don't like the noise. There is no point in making this letter too long, I have caused you enough pain already. Forgive me for burdening you, but there is one more thing I want to ask of you: if our bodies are found, please bury them together. Let the three of us be together. This is my last wish. Please do your best to see it through! Except for that, be happy! Just bear in mind that I had no other solution. Do not blame yourself. You are young, you will get married and you shall carry on the seed of our father. I decided not to write to father.

Something stops me from doing that. Goodbye, dear brother! Do not forget me, but what must be, must be, and one must go all the way through. I will do this! And one more thing, please: send Pedro the letter and the jewels."

To Pedro:

"You were my fiancé for one year. We never lied to each other, and I am grateful. You know that I love Luis de Luso, but that is not all. I am expecting his child. How could I possibly marry you? Maybe I am a coward, but I do not wish to face dishonor; I prefer peace and tranquility. You, though, have someone who is waiting to call you husband, so run, run to her! You are fortunate! Just compare yourself to me, and you will realize it. I did not dare to confront my father, but you must do that, for my sake. Marry your lover and raise your child. And do not forget me. Keep a thought for me in your heart, and pray for me, for Luis and our baby. Goodbye!"

Luis's letter to his family:

"My beloved ones, I have loved Lucia de Sousa y Monterro ever since I met her last year. It was a year during which we hid our love, for she was engaged to Pedro de Cantarra. I do not consider myself guilty for this, for Pedro knew all along about our love. Lucia de Sousa, my sweetheart, was to be married in a short while, and I would not see her anymore or very rarely. This is far too cruel for both of us – not to mention that Lucia was mine, completely mine, and she is carrying my child. Her womb is already showing its fruit. In the last month, we made the decision to leave, both of us, to that unseen world, at least unseen by anyone who has returned. I cannot let her marry another, and this is not what she wants either, for that matter. Our action will not cause Lucia any pain – I took care of that; tonight, hand in hand, we shall jump into the Mondego. Please comfort Francisco as much as you can. He knows everything, and he is barely still alive. But we asked him to keep silent about this. He swore to us! He is not to blame for anything; in fact, he is more miserable than you are. Juana should love him. She understands his suffering, and she will know how to ease his pain. Mother, father, Catarina and Juana, I love you, and believe me when I say that this is the best decision! This is not the decision of a coward, but the decision of a strong and resolute man! Goodbye!"

CHAPTER 12

When things had settled down, Doña Alba got the chance to talk to Francisco about the Marquis de Linares.

"I know that I am in mourning, but I am asking you for permission to receive him here, to be more precise, in José's cottage. Here is the letter from Lucia; she was the one who made this reunion possible. I was faithful to your father until his death. But I did not have the courage to face my family, as Lucia did. I did not defend my love; I chose to endure. The Marquis de Linares was the one whom I loved, but my parents did not consent to our marriage. José knows it all; that is why I brought him with me from my family's house, for his words have always encouraged and comforted me."

"Lucia is an angel even from her grave. He may come, but in secrecy. I shall also have a support by my side in my grief."

"Thank you, my son, you are very kind to me!"

"I think it is only fair that now, after what has happened, each of us must look for peace as we deem fit. If the Marquis de Linares is your peace, then he may come and stay in the gardener's cottage, unseen by the world. And after the mourning period, I think it would be appropriate for you to marry him. You have been given a second chance. You can write to him."

"What support do you have?"

"I shall be making long trips to Luso. There is someone there whose kindness and gentleness comforts my suffering and makes me more peaceful, more at ease."

"Juana?"

"Maybe she is the one for me; I don't know that yet. Do not worry if I leave quite often. I need that..."

"It is all right, my son."

The appearance of the medicine man by Lucia's and Luis' grave, shouting "Curse! Curse!" had enflamed the spirits of everyone around. That medicine man was also a sorcerer, the village inhabitants claimed.

People started talking about their own deaths on that very Whit Sunday, which was not exactly a Christian thing to do. Rumor had it that the families of those two were now cursed.

People were quite sure that two lovers had assuredly turned into ghosts or other evil spirits and would begin haunting the village. The peasants remembered that the medicine man had said that for two hundred years, Luis would meet Lucia for only one week, beginning only on a Whit Sunday. Then, surely, they would come out of their grave and haunt the whole area, river, castle, forests. The peasants promised themselves to be extremely careful every year on that Holy Day. Furthermore, the Bishop had married them after their deaths. What did that mean? The people continued to wonder about that, for that was not an ordinary thing; that was undeniably sacrilegious. And then the Count had died. He was criticized and condemned for not having realized, as a parent, that he was doing something wrong, that he was doing great harm.

All those words and rumors reached the castle, frightening Doña Alba. She vaguely remembered that man, chased away from the cemetery with stones. Was that even true? She prayed that it wasn't. Sorcerers should be burned at the stake and not allowed to spread evil words and curses around.

She was waiting for Rodrigo, for he was the only one who could take her out of her mood. She had received a letter from him. He was due to reach Santa Cruz any minute. José was to let her know when Rodrigo arrived. Perhaps with another man around, Francisco would be comforted sooner. He went quite often to Luso, where he was well received. But he did not learn about Luis's last wish. Only Luis's family knew about his wish for Juana to marry Francisco.

Juana took long walks with Francisco, and she was a good listener. She did not do this out of any obligation, not at all. Her brother's words were not forcing her into anything. But she could not forget Francisco's expression at the funeral, and his hand holding hers. Sometimes they would just sit on a bench without saying a word. Other times, he would pick flowers and give them to her without saying anything. What was the point of words? Juana knew how to listen even to Francisco's silence. She was a bit shy, and Francisco understood her perfectly.

One day, he reached Luso earlier than usual and found them at the table. He apologized. Juana stood up from her chair, took him by the hand like a child and had him sit next to her. She asked for another place to be set. And she said to him reassuringly:

"You are part of the family, aren't you?" Count de Luso answered for Francisco:

"My son, you belong to us! What is troubling you?"

"I do have something on my soul, Dom Joaquim."

"Tell us, we're your family!"

"People say we are cursed and that the de Sousa castle is haunted. But it is not," Francisco blurted out. Impatiently pushing the chair aside, he knelt down before Juana.

"Juana, do you believe this? Would you marry me? I... I have come to love you. I am alive only when I come to Luso. I know we have to observe this long period of mourning, but after that, we can be married. Do you believe in ghosts? Can I hope?" Juana and Dom Joaquim gently lifted him up.

"My sweet child, you have found a new father! Juana does not believe in ghosts, shadows of her brother and her sister-in-law. I wholeheartedly entrust her to you," the Count responded.

The Countess de Luso was crying openly. The servant remained with the plate in his hands.

"Water?" he murmured.

"Yes, please, Francisco needs some," Juana replied. She handed him the glass herself.

"And I want to marry you! May God forgive me, but I was waiting for you to say that. I love you, too!"

Count de Luso said that they would all go to the de Sousa castle as soon as possible.

"And we shall become engaged there, without any strangers knowing about it. We shall prove to everyone that there are no curses," Francisco declared.

"Now that we have all calmed down, can we eat?" Juana asked, clearly happy.

Francisco kissed her hands. The Countess de Luso closed her eyes; it felt as if the black of mourning had lifted from their clothes and their souls.

At the de Sousa castle, the guest in the gardener's cottage had settled in. José was glad to move into a room in the castle, thus making room for Doña Alba and her renewed love.

Thus, Francisco came to know the Marquis de Linares and found him rather charming. He was pleased to share with them his love for Juana, a shared and accepted love. He told them about the coming visit of the de Lusa family to their castle, on the occasion of their engagement.

Doña Alba gave her son the family engagement ring and a set of jewels.

"I received them when I became engaged to your father. Now a new Countess de Sousa must wear them!"

"In fact," the Marquis intervened, "you shall soon receive a new ring. We too shall be married after the mourning period." Doña Alba pressed his hands affectionately and thanked him with her eyes.

CHAPTER 13

The next week, the de Luso family came to Santa Cruz of Coimbra. They were received with joy and anticipation. They wanted to confirm the engagement between Francisco and Juana. What was the point in waiting? In one more year, they could marry. To them, it was important for their relationship to become official; nobody cared about the party.

Juana happily received the ring and the jewels. She was joyful, and so was Francisco. Then they went out in the park.

"Do you ride? Francisco asked her.

"Yes, of course. I often go riding on my little horse."

"Would you like to go to the river? You could take Lucia's horse. Or maybe you are afraid?"

"No, Francisco, I am not afraid! It is the place where they loved, they were happy only there. It is a blessed place, under no condition cursed. As I can see, our destinies are related to the river of Mondego. We can go there now, if you want!"

"We just need to saddle the horses."

"Then I'll wait for you in the parlor."

"All right, I'll be there as soon as I can." Then Juana went back in the house.

"We are going to ride," she said. "Francisco is getting the horses and will be right there. We are going to ride by the river. We don't see anything bad in doing that."

"You go ahead for a ride; the weather is lovely," Count de Luso said.

"And you can also stay here overnight. There is plenty of room for everybody. What do you say?" Doña Alba asked.

"Yes, I think we can stay," Count de Luso replied.

"May I see Lucia's room?" Juana asked.

"Yes, why not? Francisco will show it to you when you come back from your ride," Doña Alba said.

After a short ride, Juana and Francisco got off their horses and started walking.

"All this will be yours soon!"

"Yes, I like it all! Your domain is truly wonderful!"

When they reached the river, they stopped. The Mondego was flowing smoothly, as it had been for so long. Nothing had changed.

"You know, Francisco, I do not feel restless at all when I am by the river. I think that their souls are at peace now. Yet I remember that sorcerer. I wonder why…"

"Probably Luis asked for those powders lying to the old man. And he took his revenge. He said something about two hundred years and only on a Whit Sunday."

"Maybe it is then that they will come back here, Francisco! Do you think so?"

"It is possible, but I will not get scared! This is my sister and my brother-in-law and friend we are talking about! And then we don't necessarily have to come here at that time of the year. What is important is that you will be there by my side, and life goes on. We shall have children, and we shall be blessed."

"Yes, you are right. Let's go back now. Your mother has allowed me to see Lucia's room. I want you to show it to me!"

They rode back slowly, with small steps. The horses were tired, but Francisco and Juana were fully enjoying the peace surrounding them and the entire universe enfolding two people in love in that world of their own, intangible for others.

"Lucia's horse is accepting me; that means he will be mine!"

"Indeed," Francisco said.

When they entered Lucia's room, Juana noticed that nothing had changed. There were flowers in the vases, the furniture dusted. Lucia's things were everywhere.

"Mother decided to leave the room as it was. She did not change a thing. She did not throw away a thing. She comes here from time to time and just lies down in Lucia's bed. This is one of the most beautiful, bright, and radiant rooms in the whole castle."

Meanwhile, Doña Alba accepted Dom Rodrigo's proposal, but with no witnesses. She just showed Francisco her new ring, the one she was wearing instead of the family ring she had given to Juana. They had only to wait for winter and spring to pass before they could be married.

The two families and the Marquis de Linares had decided to hold the two weddings on the same day, with no fuss or glamor. Even Juana, who was getting married for the first time, agreed to this. Nobody paid attention anymore to the small things that they once valued. The spiritual union of heart and soul was far more important than anything else.

Two weeks before the two weddings, the bans were announced at Mass, and they displayed the common proclamation of the two events. The people were amazed to learn the news during the Mass that Sunday. They kept looking towards the seats of the families involved in that announcement. But who cared?

The families had waited for a whole year, according to the rule, so no one could find fault on that score. Juana had chosen a cream-colored dress, simple yet beautiful. She made herself a coronet of thyme and stitched it to the veil. Doña Alba had chosen a blue dress, for she had been married before; also she did not wear a veil, but a hat, over the simple hairstyle.

Everyone was present on the wedding day at the church. Nobody living around the area missed this special event. When the Mass was over and the four of them were married, a sigh of relief could be heard. People had accepted the union between the two families.

Doña Alba decided to move to Lisbon and start a fresh new life there. In Santa Cruz, the new couple should be alone. With tears in his eyes, Francisco accepted and understood that.

After the Marquis and Marquise de Linares left for Lisbon, the castle belonged to the young Count and Countess de Sousa y Monterro only. They had come to love each other more and more every day. Soon, Juana became pregnant and gave birth to a healthy and vigorous little boy. He became the jewel of the castle with the two aigrettes. Day by day, he was becoming more and more like Francisco. After the birth of the child, the Marquis and Marquise de Linares came to visit more frequently. Finally a heir, a child who would jump about everywhere, for the future was his – the future Count de Sousa.

There were two things that darkened the life of the families then more united than ever. First, the death of José, whom everyone considered an honorable member of the family, and who was buried in the crypt of the family. His last moments were peaceful, for his great desire was to have everyone around him. Then, after Francisco had promised him that the next gardener would care for his flowers, José also added that he was content, and he was going to join Luis and Lucia. Everybody cried over the faithful servant; his whole life had been dedicated to those he served.

The second thing that saddened the family was the reaction of peasants in the village. They were saying that the sorcerer's curse on the de Luso domain was already happening. They said that on Whit Sunday, for one whole week, they would see the two, the Count and the Countess de Luso, walking on the bank of the river, with a small child in their arms. They say that the child is crying so much that the parents cannot quiet him. It is certain that they will come every year during the week of Pentecost. They are forced to, because of the sorcerer who cursed them not to find their peace. During that time of the year, the peasants would seldom go to the river of Mondego; no one dared pass by there, except for the shepherds and their sheep. They didn't react to the curse, maybe because they were the ones who found the two bodies. At night, standing by the sheep, they would hear the child the most clearly of all, but they were not frightened; on the contrary, they talked about the suffering of the three of them and the fact that the sorcerer must be caught and taken before the Holy Chair of the Inquisition. Maybe then the three of them would find their peace.

The people at last came up with an idea. They would look for the medicine man's house in the forests around Luso. They soon found him, and it seemed as if he had been expecting them.

"Have you come to take me? I am ready!"

"Undo the curse you bound the Count and Countess de Luso with!"

"Never! They will endure it until the year 1850, and then they will find their peace. You can take me to the Bishop, to have me burned at the stake in the square. Luis de Luso lied to me, so he must pay for it!"

"And you will pay for it, too!"

"Very well," he said. "I shall feel nothing!"

"You are a devil!"

And yes... his burning was truly a spectacle. The sorcerer made no cry of pain; he only uttered the same curse we told you about.

"He was truly a devil, this man," one could hear people saying everywhere, on every street corner in Coimbra.

But the curse remained and his story was repeated year after year, although the de Luso and de Sousa families did not pay attention to such things. They lived their life in an ordinary fashion, and there was no need for a change.

CHAPTER 14

Years went by, making room for other generations. As the Mondego flows, so do people's lives, sometimes smooth and then other times, agitated. But time passes, and so does everything – joy, sorrow, pride, and vanity. All of that dies out with each second that indiscriminate time swallows up.

The deaths of the Marquis and Marquise de Linares were painful. Dom Rodrigo was first, and then Doña Alba was alone again, but only for a short time. But she did not go back to Coimbra. She wouldn't travel anymore, for journeys were severely tiring for her. Her children would come to see her; they were adults now. Her loneliness was eased when Paulo, the son of Juana and Francisco, decided to study in Lisbon. The new Marquis de Linares very seldom visited. He hadn't come there since his father passed away. He asked Doña Alba to remain in his father's palace only because he had no business in Lisbon and did not want the manor to be empty. Doña Alba thanked him for leaving her with the memories dear to her heart. She would not live long without her beloved marquis.

Paulo de Sousa y Monterro was living in the de Sousa palace in Lisbon, just as his father had done in his youth, and he would stay there all by himself, but not only in the library. He was using several rooms. He was a modest man like his father, kind in nature. Thanks to his grandmother, he had moved into society and sometimes noblemen's parlors; they welcomed him there often because of his open spirit, but especially because of his way of reading poetry. Always, he was accepted with open arms any time he came or returned.

Doña Alba passed away about six months after the death of her second husband, the marquis. She was buried next to him. The family wanted to bring her to Coimbra, but her greatest wish was to be by Rodrigo forever. Francisco accepted her decision and thus resigned himself. He returned to Coimbra together with his wife, his dear Juana. They had no more children after Paulo.

After his grandmother's death, Paulo plunged even more into studying, waiting for the holidays. He studied agriculture because he wanted to give new life to the land at Sousa.

One morning, when he did not any classes at the University, the servant brought him an invitation. Dom Pedro de Cantarra wanted to meet him and had invited him to come to his palace whenever he wished. "Who is this Dom Pedro? Should I go?" Paulo quickly wrote a note in which he let the baron know that he would arrive in two hours. The servant immediately took the note to the one who was waiting for the reply.

Dom Pedro de Cantarra, whom we know as the fiancé of Lucia and then the happy husband of his child's mother, had been fortunate all his life. Besides their firstborn, about whom the reader already knows, they had another child, a girl, Amelia de Cantarra, beautiful as a fairy and a great lover of music. Piano was her life, and actually, she was about to make her debut in society a few months later. She was not nervous about that. Since she was an optimistic sort, she thought she would survive that, too, and then she would go home. She was not interested in the goal of most young ladies – to come out in society, primarily to have a brilliant marriage.

Two hours later, Dom Pedro was standing in front of Paulo, studying him. The latter, a bit confused, was waiting for an explanation from his host.

"I have been looking forward to this meeting; maybe you are surprised about that. I was Lucia's fiancé once – you know, your aunt, the Countess de Luso. I suppose you know this family story."

"Oh, then you are something of a family member."

"I did not stay in touch, to my shame. Lucia was a saint; I owe her my happiness today. Later on, I didn't think I was worthy of her family. Here is her last letter; you will understand a great deal more after reading it. I was not a saint, but she opened my eyes. I shall be grateful to her all my life. She is always in my prayers." Paulo read that time-stained letter.

"Thank you for showing this to me!"

"Doña Alba passed away, and I know that you are now living by yourself in the de Sousa palace. If you wish, the doors of my home will be open for you from now on, any time of the day. I have two children: a boy, my elder child, who got married, and an eighteen-year-old daughter, who will make her debut soon. From what I have heard, you enjoy reading and reciting poems, and I would really enjoy it if you could come and visit us. Amelia, my daughter, is in love with poetry and music. She is always dreaming just like a turtledove. I would like for you to meet her. She does not go out often; she prefers playing the piano, and she is rather reclusive. Would you like to meet her?"

"I would like that very much; I rarely go to parlors. I'd rather wait for holidays, to go to Coimbra. I just sit by the river, and sometimes I go riding. You know, some people say about my aunt that she is a ghost. But I have never seen her on a Whit Sunday. It is true that I remain home at night; I do not go out on the bank of the river. But people do talk as if that had happened yesterday. The castle is not haunted, at any rate. My father lives there on a permanent basis, and he has never seen anything."

"Dom Francisco, if only I had listened to him ... but I didn't. Perhaps Lucia would still be alive."

"There is no point in thinking about it, or reopening old sores."

"I think you are right. You are truly wise, my young friend! Will you come to visit us?"

"Certainly."

"Why don't you come over at lunchtime? You will meet Amelia. Maybe you two will become friends."

Thus their discussion ended and Paulo went home, thinking about the family of the Baron de Cantarra. He wrote to his father, telling him about the invitation and about Pedro's daughter Amelia. He promised to keep him posted, and share all his impressions with him.

That is how Dom Francisco learned from his most recent letter that he was in love with Amelia and that she shared his feelings. He learned how wonderful, sweet, and beautiful she was, that she was witty, that she loved poetry and playing the piano. Paulo also told him that he no longer frequented parlors; instead, he would go to the Baron's house every day, and the Baron agreed to their relationship. "Father, I am in love, and I would propose to her if I had more courage, but I think I need you in this!" Dom Francisco started to laugh.

"Juana, come and read this!" Juana drew the conclusion that that would be a true wonder.

"It is as if, through her death, Lucia found the key to all problems," said Juana. "We must go to Lisbon. I shall give him the engagement ring, and I shall choose a jewel. We shall be there by his side when he proposes to her. We shall give him courage, and thus there will be more of us in Santa Cruz. Maybe we will also have grandchildren, who knows? Francisco, write to Dom Pedro and share our intention with him. Then, write to Paulo, too, and let him know to expect us!"

Their marriage took place after a very short engagement. Thus, the Sousa castle became Amelia's house. This marriage was a happy one, blessed by three beautiful children who ran in the park, with their nurses never managing to catch them.

They still lived in the castle, as if to show people living nearby that there was no curse, even though every year, there was someone who would start talking about it around Whit Sunday. At any rate, the emotional impact was decreasing, seeming more and more to be a mere legend.

But around 1850, the year when the second part of this story begins, the castle was no longer occupied. The Count de Sousa – we don't know exactly which one, for we lost track – preferred living in a palace in the middle of Coimbra. The castle was very well managed and perfectly preserved, and only three servants lived there, who did not complain of ghosts or the legend of the two-hundred-year curse.

In fact, people had changed since the Inquisition had ended and no longer put pressure on them. They were free, people said.

PART II

CHAPTER 1

Around 1840, Count Frederico de Sousa y Monterro, the young heir of the ancient family castle, married Maria de Guzman, whose father was a nobleman and whose residence was forty leagues, about 140 miles, from Coimbra. They had married for love, and their marriage promised to be filled with happiness.

Ten years later, Dom Frederico was thirty and had had a fairly peaceful life. He had married young, so it could almost be said that he grew up with his children. The five members of the family lived in a small palace in the center of Coimbra. For them, that was more comfortable than living in the old castle with its thick walls. It is true that the maintenance of the palace in the center of Coimbra was quite expensive, and of course they had a carriage and horses. All kinds of people came to visit them, so their position in society demanded this lifestyle.

The castle was perfectly preserved, but it was becoming quite an expense for Frederico. Though his business was doing well, his expenses matched his income, leaving no extra. His children were growing up and needed education, and his wife loved dresses and glamorous things. Her parlors were the most splendid in the whole city. People were proud to be invited to the de Sousa palace. And that really pandered to his vanity, but also touched his purse.

In the past few years, he had given more attention to the castle, though to the detriment of the grounds. They hadn't had a gardener for quite a long time, and only two servants of the former three remained. They did what they could to manage and take care of the grounds. They would pull the weeds that spread everywhere; they would cut the grass before it turned into a jungle. José's cottage was now surrounded by weeds, all kinds of bushes, and tall grass, so that one could barely squeeze in.

Doña Maria wanted to see the castle, but Dom Frederico hesitated. His whole family's legacy was there, his roots were there, even if nobody lived there anymore. Every little corner reminded him of his heritage.

Sometimes Dom Frederico would come alone to visit. He would go to every single room. He would open a cupboard door, which squeaked from neglect; he would go up to the attic where his ancestors' things lay under covers. He would gaze at the furniture, once so fashionable, and sigh.

Doña Maria had never visited the castle, and she wouldn't let the children go, either. They were different, they belonged to a different generation; only he, Dom Frederico, though himself changed, could still feel the call and cry of the family in his blood. He would also go to the cemetery by himself, taking one of the servants from the castle and together they would clean off the graves of long departed souls, marked by blackened, moss-covered crosses. He did not hesitate to clean them next to the servants, for he felt close to his family when he looked at the names of all those women and men from his past. He was a romantic, a melancholic. Doña Maria was the more practical of the two. Dom Frederico also liked the picture of the two aigrettes on the main door. They were part of himself, and he was proud of that heritage, but he was the only one who understood that.

Since the Inquisition had been abolished, many Jewish families had moved to the large, beautiful city of Coimbra. The Mondego River, with its special charm, also attracted many people.

That is how one of those many Jews, the wealthy banker David Lieberman, moved into a big house close to the Count's home. Lieberman had opened a branch of his bank in Coimbra, a bank that was then spreading to the largest cities in Portugal. The banker had chosen Coimbra for his residence because of the peace and tranquility and the restful walks he took on the riverbank. He was not drawn to Porto or the capital, not at all – they were crowded with people from everywhere. Coimbra was the place he enjoyed the most.

The banker had been married for a long time to his wife Rosa. She had learned to read her husband without a word being uttered. She was a kind woman for whom motherhood provided her greatest fulfillment. She was devoted to her husband, but only when she was needed. They had three children: a boy named Maxx, who was the pride of his father, and two girls, Anna and Miriam, whom their father wanted to "give away" by finding them good husbands. Maxx was the only one who truly mattered to him. His daughters were just numbers when counting people at the dinner table, but their dowries were a constant headache for him. Nonetheless, he had to have them marry well. To him, even if it hurt to pay for that, prestige was very important.

One day, he went for a walk with Maxx.

"My dear Maxx, do you know what I thought of? We could use a house somewhere in the countryside, not far from Coimbra, where the girls and your mother could spend their time as they please, and then you and I could relax after a long day at work."

"That is a good idea, father; have you heard of anyone willing to sell their house in the area?"

"No. Not yet. This is something I have just thought of. I like the castles by this river very much; there is something special about it. I just wanted to share this idea with you first. What do you think?"

"I will say again, I think it is a wonderful idea; I mean, we could go riding, we could have a garden. But isn't it too expensive for you?"

"Son, that doesn't matter. A property is a property."

"You are right, father, maybe we will get lucky. The girls and mother will be quite pleased. And I won't have to stay closed inside the house anymore."

"Yes, we will have to tell them about it tonight. They will be thrilled to be able to run around like billy goats."

"Is business going well, father? Are you happy in Coimbra?"

"Yes, even better than I expected. I like this city, and they have accepted the bank very well. I was a little bit nervous about it at first, but I am confident that we are on the right track here."

That night, during the dinner, the banker told them about his walk with his son.

"I intend to buy a house there. You will love it, ladies, and you will gain some color. Here, you look like flowers that need water. You will be able to move about more, to go out in the fresh air, to go for a walk in nature, in parks. My son and I will have a great deal of work to do in Coimbra, and thus we will be able to devote our full attention to business."

To hear him speak, it seemed as if Maxx was his son only, and Mrs. Lieberman had only the girls. But despite the banker's partiality, everyone accepted him and did not hold any grudge against him.

Maxx loved his sisters and mother. He did not share the apparent feelings of his father, who deep down in his soul loved his whole family, of course; it was only that, for him, women had no value. Maybe that was why Mr. Lieberman wished to have his girls marry well, a concern that pressed on him constantly.

After dinner, the father would always shut himself up alone in the library. Nobody disturbed him there. The rest of the family moved to the parlor.

"This is indeed a good idea, but what has got into him now?" the mother asked, a bit surprised.

"Today, we went for a walk by the Mondego. He has his mind set on buying a house near the river."

"Are there any vacant houses? I know there are some belonging to some former noblemen; I hope he gets a chance at one of them."

"And I can put my piano in a room where father won't hear it," Miriam said, laughing.

"And I want a room where I can paint at ease, without anyone coming in and disturbing me. Maybe I could also paint outside," Anna said.

Everybody started laughing.

"I can already see myself a chatelaine," the mother said. "I can see that you two have all kinds of plans and are already daydreaming. I think I could plant some flowers. Do not forget, though, that all of this depends on your father's whims."

That night, everyone went to bed with something new to think about. When all was quiet, the banker slipped discreetly out of the library, as if it were not his own house, and went upstairs to his room. He immediately fell asleep.

CHAPTER 2

As we mentioned before, David Lieberman settled down in Coimbra and opened a branch of his bank, which was bringing him quite a profit. His bank had branches in different areas of Portugal. He had appeared like grass from the earth. Nobody knew much about him; judging by the name, some people thought he was Prussian, while others thought he had come from the land of the Jews. They all spoke very well of him and minded their own affairs, without much fuss. Actually, his good reputation as a serious businessman drew a fine, select clientele eager to avail themselves of his services. Consequently, people in Coimbra frequently had business to conduct at the offices of that bank, which pleased Lieberman greatly for two reasons: one, because his profit was increasing, and second, in particular, because he could learn about prospective houses for sale in the countryside near Coimbra.

To that end, he drew up a list and started exploring the area. He visited several houses, but his heart was captured by the castle of de Sousa y Monterro. The servants told him that only the two of them lived there now. They received him downstairs on the ground floor, and then showed him the park that had become lush and overgrown, abounding in wild vegetation, growing and covering the paths, giving the sensation of being in a huge, endless field. The banker did some mental calculations and decided that he could afford to buy it. The women could live there permanently. He would restore the park, too, and the house in Coimbra would be peaceful and quiet, occupied only by men. Mostly just himself, actually, because Maxx would certainly want to live here, at least from time to time. Naturally, he would also come here whenever he pleased; it was not as if he were buying a castle exclusively for his ladies.

The servants said that they did not think the building was for sale, for they had heard nothing of the kind from the Count who had visited there only a few days before. The banker also asked whether the nobleman was wealthy or in want of funds, rather in narrow means. People told him the Count was a bit in narrow means, but not significantly, for the Count's business allowed him to maintain the palace and his family in Coimbra, as well as to preserve that castle as much as he could. Lieberman also learned that the Count's wife, Doña Maria, had never come to the castle, and that she was educating her children in Coimbra, so they considered that they belonged there, in the city of Coimbra, and not here.

The family didn't come to the castle, the servants reported – only the Count in whom that spirit of nobility remained; he would come and walk around the castle, through the park, then to the small house near the gate, and then he would clean the graves of people from his family with his own bare hands; he would not neglect the castle. Doña Maria would have given that up quickly for her comfort in the city.

"I see," the banker said to himself, "this one is a sentimental attachment! It will be difficult, but maybe I will have a better chance if I approach the wife. I want this castle for my prestige and the prestige of my business. I will find a way! I believe that this nobleman may be in rather narrow circumstances; I shall inquire about him and his family."

The banker did not make his inquiries directly, but instead, he had someone observe the house. He learned that Doña Maria was rather prodigal, that she loved luxury, and that she would receive guests on Thursdays. He also learned that they had three children, which meant many expenses, just as in his case, in fact – and then he sighed, for his children were almost grown. And he also learned that the de Sousa nobleman was an absent-minded type who loved the bird coat of arms and name, and that he lived modestly. He was not interested in his wife's parties, which he attended out of complaisance. He also learned that the Count's business was going well and that he would be even more prosperous if his wife weren't such a spendthrift. "It seems that women are, after all, the key here!" he concluded after finding out everything he wanted to know. He learned what was important, namely that Doña Maria would be happier if her husband got rid of that castle that frightened her. Their title and coat of arms wouldn't have been tarnished; others sold their castles, after all. And they had that palace in the center of Coimbra; why would they need the castle with its overgrown park, a castle built around 1400 or 1500?

With all this information in hand, the banker decided to move ahead. He asked to meet with the Count and was welcomed without hesitation.

"Dom Frederico, I had the pleasure to visit your family's castle the other day. I am a straightforward man; I would like to buy it! I like it very much, and I could bring it to its former stateliness, especially the park. Your servants told me that you stop by every now and then, but your family never comes. Maybe I am taking you by surprise with my very open and sincere request, but this is how I am. Naturally, I would offer you a generous price if you agreed to sell. I apologize if you feel offended by my offer!"

"I do not feel offended, Mr. Lieberman, only surprised. It is true that I can more easily afford to maintain this house where I welcomed you, but the castle is quite fine, too. It is true that the park is not as grand as it used to be, but I am doing everything that I can in this respect. My soul is there, Sir; it is not here in the center of Coimbra, in this colorful, bespeckled society which I have never gotten used to. At the castle, I feel as if I meet people who lived there before me. I am pleased that with my own hands, I can clean their graves where they have slept for so many centuries now. But I regret that none of my children feels the way I do! The soul of this castle will die with me, whether we still own it or sell it!"

"Count, you are welcome anytime, as if it were your home; you will not feel like a stranger!"

"Thank you, but I have not seriously considered selling it. If I do, you will be the first that I shall approach, because you have the money necessary to take good care of it."

"Shall I understand, then, that this is not a total refusal, and that I can still hope?"

"No, it is not a refusal, but I have never thought about this before. But times do change quickly, and we must adapt accordingly."

"Thank you, Dom Frederico. I hope that you will come and visit me at the bank, if you change your mind."

"Yes, I give you my word, I will come to you first."

After the banker left, the Count sat down in an armchair, his eyes closed. "Should I sell the castle? Then I would have only this palace left. The aigrettes coat of arms would shine only here and not in Santa Cruz! Maria would be pleased. She has always had a practical mind. The castle remains closed with no one living in it. It just swallows up money, not a lot, but quite enough. I could bring the two servants working there to the palace; there is always a need for an extra man here. I must talk to Maria! I am not yet convinced, but she will manage to do it. After lunch, I shall have a discussion with her. It will make her happy, and I think I will be glad, too, for this will increase my business!"

After lunch, he took his wife by the hand and led her to the library.

"What is on your mind, Frederico? You've been really quiet during the meal."

"Banker Lieberman made me an offer for the castle, and that got me thinking."

"The castle? Your family castle?"

"Yes, Maria, but neither you nor the children feel tied to it. You almost never go there, and you are always in such a hurry to leave. There isn't anyone besides me who truly feels the blood rise when getting near those old walls. I am thinking about selling it; it is of no use to anybody. Mr. Lieberman promised me I could visit anytime and still take care of the graves. Also, he has the money to restore the park, and that way the castle would last longer, even if it has a different owner. He seems to be quite a down-to-earth man. Maybe we will buy another house here where our son can settle down when he gets married. The girls will have a better dowry, and better chances to marry well. My soul does not count for much unless I sacrifice it for my family."

"Frederico, you are so noble! This idea is tearing you up, isn't it?"

"I will survive, don't worry. You are always there by my side, and our children are important."

"You are right, my darling! Sell it, and let's start a new life! Years will go by, and our son will need his own house."

"And what do you suggest that I do? Go to the bank tomorrow?"

"No, let the Hebrew stew a bit; don't let him know that this is stinging you; go and see him next week. No matter how many houses he may visit, none delights his vanity more than the de Sousa y Monterro ancestral residence."

"You are right, you are always right!"

The banker became restless when he saw the week passed by without the Count knocking at his door. "He doesn't want to sell, for sure," the banker said to himself. "And how I would have enjoyed that business deal! Plus the price was above the market value!"

He was therefore very surprised when the visit of Count de Sousa y Monterro was announced one morning. He was flabbergasted, actually, and thought to himself that he had won: "These noblemen, they do not give in at first, but they do, eventually!"

"Good morning, Mr. Lieberman!"

"Good morning, Count; please have a seat! Does your coming here mean that you have changed your mind?"

"To my great shame, I must confess that I have come to sell the castle. I know my ancestors are turning over in their graves, but I have no choice. I need more capital in the future and I promised I would come to you first."

"Would you like something to drink?"

"No, thank you."

"Is the price satisfactory for you?"

"Yes, it is an unexpectedly good price."

"I promise you I will restore it, and you can come to visit anytime you want! I fully understand that it is not easy for you to do this, which is why I am making this offer."

"Thank you. I am grateful to you! In fact, the palace in Coimbra is enough for me, and my business needs some capital. My wife wants to have another house here, so the money is quite useful right now."

"I understand perfectly! You have a son to think about. A house is always a good investment."

"We can go together to visit the castle. I know you have been there before, but I will show you its true character."

"I think that is a good idea," the banker said happily.

"Then you choose the date."

"How about tomorrow afternoon?"

"That is perfect," the Count said, standing up.

Mr. Lieberman was indeed thrilled by his guide. Everything was so different. The Count took him to the attic as well, where furniture had lain under covers for centuries. The nobleman showed him the jewel that soon would no longer belong to him. The banker prized the coat of arms on the doors and decided not to remove it. The Count was thrilled.

The contract was concluded without any mention of the folklore of the region regarding the castle, although there were rumors about it. So many years had gone by, and yet rumors still lingered. It was a story passed from father to son.

CHAPTER 3

As soon as the deal was concluded, the banker brought a cadre of workers who restored the de Sousa castle. The interior was freshly plastered, the carpets were shaken out and washed, as were the blinds and curtains; the panels and everything made of wood was varnished and polished, especially the floors; the windows casements were painted; most of the furniture remained where it was, which delighted the banker. Everything spoke of the past and was so well preserved that the traces of time were merely a hallmark of elegance. The banker especially liked the stairs leading into the foyer, so he paid even closer attention to that part of the vast restoration and cleaning endeavor.

The workers had much work to do in the park, including statues and fountains as well as all the walkways and their pavement, which had seriously deteriorated. Everything was restored. The fountains were charming again; they bubbled with fresh, clear, cool water. Everything was transformed. The gardeners were living as in a verdant forest; they shaped the bushes with their sheers and planted flowers in the old flowerbeds. They even painted the benches. The place had become quite charming and delightful for a walk. Mr. Lieberman's pleasure turned into sheer bliss when he discovered the small cottage of the gardener on the other end of the park, and he thought, truly thrilled: "I wonder how many trysts took place here!"

He immediately asked the workers to restore that house, too; it had only a ground floor with two rooms, a kitchen, and a lavatory. "Here, my girls will be able to paint and sing. But that will be it! Nothing more! Look, there is a secret door! If I hadn't looked more carefully, I wouldn't have noticed it. I believe that every castle has a cottage with a secret door like this. I like this place more and more. I like that Latin motto, too. The Count will be pleased with the way I have restored it all!" The banker was talking to himself, excited and pleased with his new property.

After they removed all of the construction materials, he extended an invitation to Dom Frederico to visit the castle, to show him what he had achieved. The Count was truly amazed.

"Just like the old times," he said.

"Do you like it?"

"Very much! What about the gardener's cottage in the park?"

"I have restored it also. Would you like to see it?"

"Yes, please. The gardeners of our family lived there. You should find a lot of gardening tools inside."

"Yes, that is true; it did not occur to me that those were gardening tools. So should I carry on the tradition and let the gardener live there?"

"No, Mr. Lieberman, times have changed. These people have families in the village. Our gardeners were all alone. In a way, we were their family."

"I was thinking that my girls should bring the piano and the painting tools here and make this a spot of their own."

"This may be indeed a good place for painting, because it is quiet and the pleasant atmosphere may be inspiring, but for the piano I recommend a certain room in the castle, which has a wonderful acoustics. This house is not for music."

"Hmm, I did not think about that, about acoustics, about sonority. Please show me the room; you know it best."

They went back through the beautiful curving walkways with fine sand scattered on them; they passed the restored statues and the fountains from which water was joyfully springing.

"You can come whenever you like, Dom Frederico, as I promised you. I can see a certain nostalgia in your eyes; maybe you wish to take something from the castle, a painting, a vase, something close to your heart, or something reminding you of your childhood."

"You are very kind. Actually, I did want to ask you this favor."

"Go in the castle, wherever you wish, it is your prerogative. We really should remain friends; the world does not end here, if the castle is no longer yours!"

"Thank you once again. I am most grateful!"

The banker remained in the parlor, not interested in what the Count de Sousa would take with him. It seemed only fair to him; moreover, he was thinking about his business. The Count was not a patron of his bank, so maybe by strengthening relations between them, the banker would gain the Count as one of his clients.

Dom Frederico went upstairs to the second floor and opened a large door that no longer squeaked. It had already been greased and repaired. He entered a room facing the entry way of the castle. That had been Lucia's room. In childhood, he was never allowed to enter that room. He knew why, and he was curious to see where one of his ancestors with such a sad history lived. Many things had been taken from the room, but he noticed a painting still very well preserved. He took it off the wall and examined it slowly. On the back, it said *Lucia de Sousa y Monterro.* "This is she! How lovely she was!" Lucia was very young and very beautiful in the painting. Running his hand over the board behind the painting, he noticed that it was a bit distended. He carefully opened the clamps and discovered two bundles of letters. On one was written "Lucia," and on the other, "Luis."

"Ah! Luis de Luso!" the Count exclaimed. He put the letters back, closed the clamps, and thought about what else to take with him. He opened a drawer and found a crucifix. He took that as well. He also took a religious icon off the wall, and then he decided to leave.

Suddenly, he didn't want to be in that room anymore. He went downstairs to see the banker, to thank him and tell him goodbye. Lieberman thanked him for coming and said that he was expected to come again. He didn't even notice what the Count had taken.

Dom Frederico was thinking about the feelings he had while inside the castle, about the restlessness pressing down on him. He had felt a presence in the room, like a breeze. Pentecost comes after the Easter, he thought. At that time, Lucia will come back, as people say. But Lieberman is Jewish; he is not like those people. Frederico could hardly wait to read those centuries-old letters. Maybe he would understand what had happened.

After the Count left, the banker lingered a bit longer, giving the last orders of the day. He was pleased. They still had to bring the furniture and the servants from the other house. He thought two servants would be enough for him; it is women who generally need a host of servants around them, he thought. Then, he would come to the castle quite frequently, and the servants in Coimbra would be more like guardians.

By the end of the week, the whole family was already settled in the castle, enjoying the peacefulness there. Anna had already taken her painting tools and her easel to the small house, and Miriam had a room all to herself where she could study the piano at ease.

"We will stay here," Mrs. Lieberman said. We will not return to Coimbra again soon. You were right, darling, everything is wonderful and full of color. I like the park very much, as well as the room I have chosen!"

"We like our rooms, too," Miriam said. "They are on a rather secluded hallway and they are next to one another. Do you like your room, Maxx?"

"Yes, because it faces the front, so I will be able to see every movement in the yard and by the door."

"And you will sound the alarm," the girls said, laughing.

"I'm glad that you like the park as well as the castle and the rooms you have chosen! Rosa, the rooms chosen for us are the masters' rooms, the very rooms of the counts themselves. Maybe we too will feel a bit nobler."

"Is that so? I didn't know that," Mrs. Lieberman said, "but now I realize that it must be true, because my room has a feminine air about it, and it is connected to a boudoir, so I really have two rooms."

"You are lucky, for I have only one room, and it is not that large. I think that the Count who lived in it was rather modest."

"Father, you must settle for a small room, but we have wonderful rooms!"

"Yes, I can see that I made a good deal, even if none of my girls gave me a kiss for that, a small kiss there on the cheek."

Bursting out laughing, the girls jumped on their father, kissing him with passion, until Mr. Lieberman managed to escape and run. The banker loved his family very much, but in his own way. His wife and son were laughing out loud, now that the father was at his girls' mercy, astonished at the way he revealed his feelings – which nobody doubted. He tried to be severe and forceful, but the two cheerful girls were always conquering him, for they were his girls!

Upon hearing that the noble castle had a new owner and that the two servants had left to go to the Count's palace in Coimbra, opinions were divided. Some approved and others did not. Everyone wondered who that family was, what kind of servants they had, and how many of them there were. They learned that he was Jewish and a banker on top of that, that he had three children, and that he would not remove the de Sousa coat of arms. That was not particularly important information, but let us see what happens, they thought to themselves.

People were glad when they saw the park as it used to be, for that was a sign of prosperity. They thought that maybe, after that sale, old memories about what had happened two hundred years before would die out like leaves in autumn.

Everyone was thinking also that in a castle where people lived, there was need of food – eggs, milk, cheese, venison, and wine – and thus, they concluded, there would be some money coming out of it. Some were already thinking of how much fish they would send over to the castle kitchen, as well as of the wonderful sound of coins in their pockets. So, one after another, the inhabitants of that area wordlessly wished the new owners welcome.

CHAPTER 4

The weather was lovely at that time of the year. Not too hot, but not too chilly either. The new owners of the de Sousa castle were truly enjoying life in their new home. They had forgotten about noisy Coimbra. The girls were happily running in the park, startling the birds in the trees. They were studying music and painting, each doing what she loved most and what she did best. Watching her daughters, their mother got a certain vicarious satisfaction. She too was at last feeling freer and not so tight-laced as in the house in that large city.

They got on well with people in the village, and they bought from them everything they needed for their life in the castle. Thus, the locals were happy, too. They had employed a man from the village skilled in stable management, who reported that his masters were good, decent people.

Sometimes, the girls and their brother would stroll along bank of the river. That was a delightful view! They would wander around the area all day long, and when they came back home, they ate very well, until their mother told them they would gain weight if they went on like that. The girls would burst out laughing, and after eating, they would leave again. They were all happy, actually they were radiant. Even the banker noticed the change and affirmed that they were content. He too enjoyed walking in the park to the gardener's cottage, a secret spot, as he called it. His wife preferred to sit on a bench with a book in her hand. She was contented because others around her were happy.

Maxx was the biggest jokester of the family. He would raise the alarm from his window at any movement in the yard. He would make a boisterous proclamation about the girls' arrival, to their exasperation, for they were always startled, almost falling off their horses.

Maxx's room had a wide windowsill, which expedited his pranks and jokes; in fact, he could have comfortably slept there. On the sill, there was a cushion just the right size for him. Maxx felt sure that before he settled in that room, somebody else had used it the same way as he did. He liked his room, for he could see quite a long way from his window. He had become a frisky little boy again with blonde locks who drove his sisters crazy. He had always been a spoiled child, spoiled by everyone including his sisters. Even their father would tolerate that. Maxx was his only son, and even if he sometimes objected that spoiling the child spoiled his education, he had no choice but to accept it.

Life at the castle transformed the young people into children again, while Rosa, their mother, grew younger simply watching them. The banker was pleased; he would shrug his shoulders and go about his own pursuits. He was truly nervous when the children started playing hide-and-seek and they really had places to hide, thank God! The servants were also laughing up their sleeves. They served a family full of fun with a master who tried to pose as a serious and authoritative man, but never succeeded. The castle had come back to life just as in the old times.

One day, a minor incident brought the castle to sudden noisy laughter. Maxx had grown tired of sitting at his desk with his books, and he decided to get up on the windowsill and throw something to frighten someone. He loved to tease the cook who passed by often and who would always get scared. During the few times when she was not by the oven, she had the habit of talking to the stable man, thus passing in front of Maxx's room. He threatened to tell the banker about that, but never did.

Maxx watched her from the window and dropped a glass. The cook was taken aback at first, but the lively laughter of the young master told her where it had come from.

"Young man, do not throw my things out of the window! They must stay in the kitchen, not broken to pieces!" But she hadn't even finished her scolding when suddenly she heard a thump from the upper floor. The young man had fallen off the windowsill.

The cook shouted anxiously:

"Young Maxx, are you all right? What happened?"

"I'm fine! I just laughed so hard, I fell off the window."

"Thank goodness you did not fall outside," the woman said, picking up the pieces of glass. "I hope this will teach you a lesson. Did you hurt yourself?"

"No, I just broke a bit of the sill, and I got caught on a nail. I'll get a hammer and fix that."

"You be careful, for this castle was not built yesterday. I hope from now on you will stay still."

"I promise. Pffffff, it falls down, all of it!"

"We'll fix that somehow, and get it back in place. Christian, the gardener, will help you with that."

"I can do that myself," Maxx said as if he had lost his voice. "You may go now, I will get back to work; I won't scare you anymore."

"Good," the cook said, going back to her pots.

Lost his voice!? Not at all! That was just a voice of amazement. Under the windowsill, strategically placed so as not ever to be discovered, Maxx found a diary belonging to a girl, judging by the handwriting. It was very well preserved, although time-stained, and the handwriting was energetic and pointed. "What a good place for hiding things!" Maxx thought. "If I had not fallen down from the window, and caught on the nails, this notebook would never have been discovered. So a girl used to live here. It looks like I've chosen a girl's room. Probably, just like I do now, she must have seen before anyone else when a carriage came or a hunting party returned." He was astonished by his discovery.

With great care, as if he were a thief in his own house, he locked the door to his room and opened the diary. "Today is the 30th of April, 1649, and it is my birthday. My name is Lucia and I am the second child of Count Felipe de Sousa y Monterro and his wife, Doña Alba. I received a pony for my birthday, as a present, and I am going to take him for a ride by the river. Thus, I shall have a lot of exercise, which will also make me tired. Francisco is my elder brother and he goes to school in Lisbon. His best friend is the son of Count de Luso, Luis...." He heard somebody knocking at his door. Maxx jumped as if he had been burned. He quickly hid the notebook and hurried to the door.

"Who is it?"

"It's me, Christian; I brought a hammer and some nails to fix the window. The cook told me that you fell down and broke the sill loose."

"Just a second!" Maxx opened the door and the gardener entered with his tools.

"Ah, it's no big deal; the sill just loosened a little. The nails have weakened over time, so please do not get up on it again. It is not safe."

The stable man went about his business, but all the family gathered around.

"What is going on here?" his mother asked.

"Nothing much, just the windowsill fell," Maxx replied.

"And you fell too, right? Did you hurt yourself?"

"No, mother, I'm fine. Christian will mend it and I will lose my favorite spot. I shall not climb up there anymore. They replaced the woodwork in this castle, but they forgot about the windowsill. Or who knows? Maybe I have put on some weight, for I enjoy everything here! Right, mother?"

"Yes, son, everything is wonderful here, like a fairytale; I believe that truly good people used to live here. If you are all right, then I am going. Christian is almost done here."

After everything was fixed, Maxx started reading the diary again. It was not a large notebook. The girl wrote little, and not every day. The diary became interesting when her father arranged her engagement to Pedro de Cantarra while she was in love with Luis. He was very touched by her description of love, especially where Lucia wrote that there was another life pulsing inside her and that she was desperate because she could not belong to Luis. The girl was seized by the fear that her notebook would be discovered, which was why she thought that the spot under the window would be a safe place to hide it forever.

"That was until I found it!" Maxx said to himself, rubbing his elbow, now a bit sore from the fall. He felt fear and restlessness when eventually, the two lovers decided to throw themselves into the Mondego. The diary ended abruptly, with the words being sketched nervously. Lucia was praying for God to forgive her for the soul of her child. She signed it and wrote down the year 1650, but no date, she just wrote: Whit Sunday 1650.

Maxx closed the notebook, thinking about that miserable girl who loved to climb on the windowsill, just as he did. Did they do it? Did they drown in the river of Mondego? According to the writing, she seemed to have an impulsive personality, so it was possible. He was not afraid to live in the room of the miserable girl. On the contrary, he felt sympathetic toward her. This year was two hundred years since the last date written in the notebook. "I must try to find out more about this; I want to understand this. Soon we will have the Catholic Pentecost Holy Days. I shall go to the kitchen; I can always find some busybodies there, especially Eufrasia, the cook," he told himself, already determined to solve the mystery revealed in the notebook he had found. He went down to the kitchen and started asking the cook a lot of questions:

"Eufrasia, you are very old; what do you know about Lucia de Sousa y Monterro?

Eufrasia dropped the plates and prayed he would not ask her more.

"Look, you are breaking dishes, too! Is there something serious that you don't want to tell me about? It is only me, I won't tell anyone, I promise!"

"How do you know about her, Mr. Maxx?"

"You know that I fell and broke the windowsill. Well, under the wood was her diary, where she told about a tragedy. She said she was going to throw herself into the Mondego together with her lover, so that she wouldn't have to marry a baron."

Eufrasia crossed herself and pulled Maxx closer to her. She told him hesitantly about the curse, the spirits, and that this year it would all be over, for it had been two hundred years since then.

"It will be over at Pentecost? That's what I'm thinking. Everything will happen that week!"

"Yes, master! A little more time and they will find their peace. Please swear to me that you will not frighten your mother and sisters!"

"I promise, I give you my word. You will be the one who will tell them the story. Not me, ever!"

"Master, show me the notebook!"

"Come with me, it is hidden in my room." Eufrasia followed him silently. "Here it is!" Eufrasia looked at the notebook, but barely touched it.

"You know, something really makes me nervous; I think she will come looking for it. She can feel that it is no longer in its place. Unreconciled spirits have all kinds of senses."

"She will come on Whit Sunday," Maxx said. "Let's wait until then for the Countess de Luso!"

"Master, do not talk like that! This is serious!"

"And I am as serious as I can be, Eufrasia! I am not playing. She will come, I am sure of that!" Eufrasia crossed herself and left the room without saying anything else.

"Eufrasia! Only the two of us know about this, remember!" That was all she could still hear.... "We will watch this together!"

The closer Whit Sunday got, the more often the two met and talked about the legend. Maxx knew every corner of Eufrasia's kitchen. They were both curious and anxious at the same time. The morning of the first day of Pentecost, however, did not bring anything new.

"See, Eufrasia, maybe there's nothing to it."

"Yes, maybe, but souls walk at night, not in the morning."

"You are right; we shall see tonight. I have a plan. After everybody is asleep, I shall come out of my room and lock the door. Then we shall stay close to the stairs, without being seen. We will see if she comes".

"I just hope my heart can stand that, master!"

"It will. We will be together. We are in this business together."

"Yes, Sir," Eufrasia mumbled, making the sign of the cross a thousand times.

The day went by without incident. The girls took care of their own amusements, laughed a lot, went for a walk until they grew tired, and then had dinner together with the whole family. Thus night came quickly for them. After eleven o'clock in the evening, Maxx came out of his room, locked it soundlessly, and went downstairs to the kitchen. He found Eufrasia greatly distressed, tears in her eyes, feverishly touching the small beads of her rosary.

"Master, master, she will come! I am certain of this! What do we do?"

"I think too that she will come. We will stay hidden and watch her. We will not frighten her away, but simply observe her. Close to midnight, we will slip into the niche near the library."

They had been waiting for some time. The bells of the monastery rang at midnight. It didn't take long before a cold breeze struck them both. Through the locked door, a woman dressed in an old-fashioned style entered and started up the stairs. She was radiant like an angel. She knew exactly where she was headed and she climbed slowly with light steps, holding her long dress that seemed to hang heavy. Her hair was loose and at her neck she had a shining chain. There was a deathly silence, so the two of them could hear their hearts beating. The girl arrived upstairs and started towards her room, whose door latch she pressed in vain. She could not get in.

"Master, she enters everywhere: she get in through walls and doors, but she can't get into her own room. Look, she can't get in. You must help her!"

"Keep silent, she's coming back!"

Indeed, the girl started back downstairs. One could see that she was crying and that she was helpless. She stopped for a moment and leaned against the balustrade, then sighed as she reached the bottom, vanishing from sight as she had appeared at first. The two breathed in relief.

"How beautiful she was and what a dress she wore!" Maxx said.

"That is her wedding dress. She was supposed to marry Pedro in that dress. They buried her in it, next to Luis de Luso. The priest wedded them after their deaths and registered the ceremony as if it had happened before their drowning. Their graves are in Luso, at the castle."

"She will not come back tonight. Let's go to sleep. Tomorrow we shall leave the door locked as well, but on the third night, I shall leave it open, and I will remain in the room. I am not afraid! I like her! She is so pale and so sad!"

"Do not fall for a ghost, master! Remember, she is married!"

"Let's go to sleep, Eufrasia! We'll talk about this in the morning!"

As he climbed the stairs, Maxx got a whiff of a special perfume in his nostrils, Lucia's. The second night, Lucia came again, and again she found the door locked. She went back downstairs and sat on the steps. She began to cry; then she lingered longer, and when she realized that, she stood up quickly and vanished from sight. But the scene was witnessed by two more servants who, without knowing that they could be heard and seen, were saying that she was the drowned Lucia, and that must tell their masters about it, especially since Mr. Maxx was staying in her room.

CHAPTER 5

People in the countryside wake up at the crack of dawn, so the next morning the two servants were the first to arrive in Eufrasia's kitchen, to her amazement.

"Good Lord, what are you doing here before even tasting the morning tea?"

"Eufrasia, we saw Lucia de Luso last night and we want to tell the master about it!"

"And you want me to believe you? She's been dead for two hundred years, and this castle is not the river that she comes to. The banker will not believe you; besides, he is Jewish and doesn't believe in that nonsense! Go on, get out of here and take your lies with you!"

"But it is Pentecost, remember?"

"And I am standing with my feet in the Mondego, right? Come on, get out, you're in my way!"

The servants went out, baffled; maybe they had dreamed about Lucia's visit, but they would still let the master know about it. Eufrasia felt her heart jump out of her chest. She really had to talk to her young master. The two servants refused to leave; they were determined to wait for their master, convinced that they had indeed seen Countess de Luso. The banker was the first of the family to wake up. When he came out of his room, to his amusement, he found his two servants waiting for him by the door.

"What is it? Where is the fire? What happened? What are you coming here for, like a ghost, to trouble my day's beginning?"

"Master, that is precisely why we are here!"

"To trouble me? I'll bite your noses off immediately!"

"No, master, it is the ghost!"

"The ghost?" the banker said, astonished. "What are you talking about?"

"Master, don't be upset with us; let us tell you first and then you'll understand."

"But fast, for I don't have time for this."

"Master, the countess showed up last night, right at midnight. You know that last night was the first day of Pentecost."

"The Countess from Coimbra came last night? Why didn't you wake me up?"

"Nooo, we're talking about the ghost of the Countess Lucia de Sousa y Monterro. Two hundred years ago, they wanted her to marry a nobleman from Lisbon, but she was in love with somebody else. They both took their own lives, throwing themselves into the Mondego. The parish priest married them at their funeral, in exchange for a lot of money, dating the papers prior to their deaths. Thus the Countess de Sousa became Countess de Luso, taking the name of her husband. Some witch man cursed them to haunt the river for two hundred years. It seems that this year is the end of the two hundred years, and she has come to tell this castle goodbye."

"Really."

"Last night, she was wearing her wedding dress; she went upstairs, and tried to enter Mr. Maxx's room. That used to be her room. She could not get in, and she sat down by the stairs and started crying, and then she left."

"Listen to me carefully!" Mr. Lieberman said impatiently. "The Liebermans are not Catholic; we are Jewish, so we have nothing to do with Whit Sunday and this woman. I don't believe in that. Not to mention that the Holy See burned witches and wizards, not left them to walk around as they pleased!"

"They did burn him, master, and he felt nothing. He went on cursing these noble people."

Because of all the commotion, the doors from the other bedrooms opened, and the other four members of the family were listening to the conversation. Maxx was calm and composed, but looked rather confused. The women were of course terribly frightened.

"David," Mrs. Lieberman said, "let's leave this place! We'll be strangled in our sleep!"

"Yes, father, let's leave!"

"Silence, everybody; if this countess truly exists, she is looking for her room – that is Maxx's room. And my smart son is sleeping with his door locked, so she won't come in. And then this thing is supposed to happen only one week per year, and it ends this year, according to the legend, for it has now been two hundred years."

"Master, Eufrasia can tell you the story, too."

"What? She's not sleeping either, but haunting around at night? Maybe it was her!"

"No, master, we know her only too well. We know Lucia from the painting in her room, which the Count took along with that icon."

"Yes, I remember. What a way to begin my day! My head aches already! Tell Eufrasia to come over here."

"Yes, master, I am here. Breakfast is ready."

"Leave that and tell us about this Lucia. What's her story?"

"The countess has been wandering for two hundred years now, master, on every Whit Sunday night with Luis de Luso and their baby, by the river where they took their own lives. Maybe she wants to say goodbye or maybe she forgot something in her room. This year, the shepherds did not hear the baby crying anymore, and they haven't seen the young people either."

"Oh, my God, there's a baby, too?" Rosa asked.

"Do you expect me to believe you?" the banker said. "Well, I don't! Maxx will deal with this somehow. He won't open the door, and that will be it. She'll be gone in a few days. I don't believe any of this! And you, my ladies, you are shivering as if the Countess was there last night by your side. Eufrasia, let's eat, please, if everything is ready. I have to go to the office. I have a lot of work to do, and I don't have time for ghosts. My son will take care of that, for he is also a master here! Ah, one more thing... you are forbidden to come out of your rooms at night. Lock the door to your room and nothing will happen to you. I hope I have made myself clear! My head is aching, listen to that... ghosts here in my house! I'm hungry!"

The discussion ended abruptly, once the banker left. The women went downstairs, too, somewhat more composed and calm after seeing the master undaunted.

The servants took the young master Maxx aside, and told him one more time what they had seen, which was, actually, what he had seen, too. Maybe the last time she came, she wanted some things from her room, or maybe she knows the new masters of the castle. They took all those possibilities into account, trying in vain to make sense of Lucia's presence in the castle the night before. The servants were shivering and begging Maxx to move to another room that week.

"I'm not leaving my perfect room because of a beautiful woman! Father is right; I shall manage it somehow! I am going to have breakfast now. I woke up too suddenly this morning, and I am a bit lightheaded."

The two servants, seeing that nobody believed them, also went back to the kitchen, for they were hungry, too. Eufrasia had already started eating.

"Are you done with the ghosts?" She said, in control of herself. "You do what our master told you: lock your room. Also, I don't believe that a woman of noble descent would come to visit the servants' wing, so she has nothing to do with you, if what you saw is true and you weren't dreaming. In fact, it's your master's door handle she's pulling, not yours. Now eat quickly, for I have to send you to get some supplies from the village."

The servants shrugged their shoulders, and after they finished eating they went about their own daily business, although they were still discussing the vision they had seen the previous night. "That's why she is not by the river, for she is at her home, and she is all alone!" People seemed willing to believe that, especially after they learned that she was only trying to open the door to her room, where the young master sleeps, and that she had come in through the main door without unlocking it, but she couldn't get in through Maxx's door. "And it is Pentecost, do not forget that!" That was pretty much what the village inhabitants were saying, until by the evening, everybody in the village knew about the ghost – that she was beautiful and looked exactly like the girl in the painting, that she had her hair loose, that she was wearing her wedding dress. Everybody kept an eye on the castle, locking their doors securely. Eufrasia had a hard time finding an opportunity to talk to Maxx.

"Master, what do we do?"

"Do not worry; tonight, everybody will have their door locked, and a cupboard leaning against it."

"Yes, master, I think you are right."

"Eufrasia, I have a plan, but I will tell you about it later after dinner; right now, people might get suspicious if they see us spending too much time together. I'll talk to you later; I'll come to the kitchen!"

The cook agreed to that, nodded, and went to take care of her own chores. Over dinner, the banker asked everyone whether they had any doubt regarding the nonexistence of the ghost."

"I for one do not believe in that. This girl was Countess de Luso. She must haunt that castle, not this one. "

Everybody opened their eyes wide, and what they were trying to hide came to the surface.

"So you are afraid! Be careful, you will not digest your food well if you listen to the nonsense uttered by some ignorant people. If you would feel better, I will ask the Count de Sousa tomorrow about his ancestor. He is a man of honor; he will not lie to me. Now come back to your senses, you're already ruining my good mood! What about you, Maxx, are you afraid?"

"No, father, I am fine. Even if she comes, she can do no harm."

"That's my boy! Finally, someone with a clear mind!"

The women ate hardly anything, then moved to the parlor. They were solemn, as if the queen had passed in front of them. They were waiting for bedtime so they could go to sleep and get rid of the continuous teasing of the banker. In fact, he went to sleep first. When everybody was safely locked in their rooms, Maxx went downstairs to the kitchen. Eufrasia was putting everything back in its place as usual after dinner. She was generally the last one to go to sleep.

"Master, are you here? Nobody can hear us here. I've checked and everybody has gone to bed."

"Eufrasia, you go into the niche tonight, and I shall stay in my room, but with the door unlocked. This is my plan. Be careful not to spoil it by fainting – and keep your heart beat under control."

"Are you sure, young Maxx?"

"Yes, very sure. I am not afraid. On the contrary, this girl is so unhappy. Why not find out why?"

"You are truly brave!"

"You, too; I have never met a woman like you! You've seen my mother and my sisters; if I went now and knocked at their door, they would surely die of fright."

"God forbid, what are you saying?"

"No more talking! Make sure you are alone, and hide in the niche near the library at the proper time. I'm going to my room now."

Maxx then left the kitchen and hurried upstairs. He didn't have much time.

CHAPTER 6

The staircase of the castle, which Eufrasia was to watch, was made of walnut. Beautifully fashioned and meticulously preserved, it had endured through the centuries. Thus the banker had nothing to restore, simply to maintain. At the moment, however, he wasn't concerned about the stairs or God-knew-what countess had woken from the dead to return to her home; in fact, to be very honest about it, he slept like a baby. He had put all his worries behind him and didn't care much about the fears of others. To him, that woman should be haunting the de Luso house, for it was there that she had been married after having passed away, and that was something that seemed really strange to Mr. Lieberman, but maybe such had been the custom then.

Peace reigned over the whole house; not a sound was heard except the faint ringing of the monastery bells every quarter hour. Well, probably every half hour and on the hour sharp. Soon that hour would be midnight. Eufrasia crept into the niche, barely breathing, waiting.

Suddenly, she heard a light rustle, and Lucia de Luso stepped onto the marble slab by the stairs. She hesitated a bit, as if gathering her thoughts and deciding whether she should go upstairs or look around. The girl realized that several things had changed, but most remained the same. She was dressed the same way, in that same wedding gown, beautiful like a fairy. She was as pale as before, and her sadness was reflected in her eyes, those bright, spectral eyes from another world. She started upstairs, leaning on the balustrade and apparently listening for sounds around her.

"Who knows where she may have come from?" Eufrasia was thinking, "maybe even from the crypt of the de Luso family. She has come from far away, poor thing, but maybe she moves like a thought. She is just a soul, not a body. I wonder if she can feel me. If she looked at me, I think I would die right here on the spot!"

Eufrasia forced herself to stand still, not to do anything which might trouble the spell of Lucia's apparition. But Lucia had other plans, and yet she did seem to feel something, causing her to stop in front of the

92

stairs. "And I can't make the sign of the cross either, for I would chase her away! Also, I have to stay here until she comes out of her room – I mean Mr. Maxx's room! I wonder what he is doing," poor Eufrasia thought to herself, tormented. Pondering all of that, she managed to keep her nerves under control and her mind busy. Meanwhile, Lucia went upstairs and then headed down the hall toward her room. One could hear, as she gently pressed on the door handle, that the door opened. Eufrasia closed her eyes.

Lucia caught her breath in surprise; she had finally found the door unlocked. She pushed it and entered, silently closing the door behind her. She went straight to the window and looked outside. Then she turned and looked around the whole room. "Nothing is as it used to be," she said to herself. "And someone is sleeping in here," she realized when she came closer to the bed. "I shall sit down and stay for a while. But where is my painting with the letters? Ah, I forgot; they are in the palace in Coimbra; our successor, the current count, took it and found the bundles. But there is no danger, for he is a good man," she thought, closing her eyes.

Maxx, who anticipated this momentary restlessness, decided to get out of bed. The girl was sitting with her eyes closed, and she looked as if she were sleeping. Maxx went closer and very gently touched her shoulder. The girl was startled, but the boy was smiling so beautifully and reassuringly that she was not scared.

"Don't be afraid, please," he said. "I know you, and I've been waiting for you for so long."

"You know me? I don't even exist!"

"I've touched you, and I have felt not a shadow, but a body."

"You wanted to see if I AM?"

"I will say again... I've been waiting for you! You are Lucia. You've chosen your room well. You can see everything from here; that is why I chose this particular room. I send the alarm from here when I see something coming from a distance."

"I used to do that also, especially when I knew my brother was coming."

"Francisco..." said Maxx.

"Yes, that was his name; I tormented him quite a lot with my secrets. Aren't you afraid of me?"

"No, I told you, I have been waiting for you. I used to enjoy sitting by the window, where the sill is wider. I don't sit there anymore, because I fell off with the mattress and broke the wooden sill. Underneath it, I found a diary belonging to Lucia de Sousa y Monterro. Namely you."

"Have you read my diary?"

"Yes, all of it. It is remarkable how you fought for your love. People in the village talk about the curse uttered by a medicine man. Luis, your lover, asked him for some powders, so that it wouldn't hurt you when you jumped into the Mondego."

"Yes, that is true."

"When you were buried in the cemetery, the medicine man showed up, the one who cursed Luis for having lied to him, allegedly needing the powders for his horse, and not for you to pass away from this world. Because of that, you wandered for two hundred years by the river, and people would hear the crying of the baby. A priest wedded you after you died, upon the request of your families. So you are Countess de Luso and dressed in your wedding gown. The two hundred years have gone by. I'm thinking that maybe now you want to say goodbye to this castle. Is that true? You are so beautiful, Lucia. I have never met such a beautiful girl as you! You are pale, but that only increases your beauty. Now tell me what you are doing here and why you are alone. Since Pentecost began, shepherds say you no longer go to the river."

"It is true, we don't go there anymore. I decided to come here at night, for a short while. Like a goodbye. What you said is true, but everything will come to an end, and we shall find our peace at last. What is your name?"

"Maxx Lieberman. I am a Jew. My father has recently bought the castle, restored the park, which was quite neglected, and repaired the cottage at the very end."

"Ah, the cottage is still there! I had some wonderful moments of love there, but also moments of bitterness." Maxx took her hand in his and went on:

"My father is a banker; he has a lot of money, and Count de Sousa y Monterro already has a palace in Coimbra. The castle was not occupied, only maintained. I believe that the successor of your family was rather short on money. His wife, they say, spends quite a lot. They have three children. I don't know any more than that. I have two faint-hearted sisters, faint-hearted since they learned that you have been walking around at night. Last night, two servants saw you and spread the word in the village. But you have three allies: my father, who doesn't care, then me, and Eufrasia, who works in the kitchen. And we were hiding in there! You've come for two nights in a row. You got in through the locked door to the castle, but you could not get into your room. I had locked it before. On the third night, we decided to leave it open. You had such a sad face that you convinced us. So what is weighing on you?"

"Where is Eufrasia?

"She is downstairs. She saw you enter while I was waiting for you here, as you can see. Please tell me what is wrong."

"That curse you told me about," Lucia started talking, withdrawing her hands from his, "was like hell to us." She pressed her hands to her face and continued. "I could see Luis and the baby only at Pentecost, for one single week; the rest of the time, I would just be there by myself, as in a void, waiting. If only they had let me be with my little boy, but no, somebody decided that he should be with my husband. The baby was always crying so hard because he didn't want to be apart from me. And yet he had to. This year will be the first that we can spend together; we shall not be apart anymore. That is why we are no longer heard or seen by the river. I am waiting for them here at the castle. They will not come in; they will just come to get me. But I don't know exactly when that will be."

"Maybe after the Pentecost is over?"

"Maxx, I will come not only this week, but all the time, until Luis comes for me!"

"And what do you do during the day?"

"I sit in a void, where nobody can see me. I leave from where I come every year. In that place, it is only oneself and one's own conscience. It's all quiet there; I can sense only my thoughts and my soul's pain."

"Does it take you long to get here?"

"No, a mere second. I think that I have to go now."

"But tell me, what are you looking for? A book?"

"No, I'm not looking for anything physical, only my memories; I'm looking for my life. I lived only here, not anywhere else. I was only seventeen when these things happened!"

"And doesn't it upset you to know that you died so young?"

"No, I told you, where I go, it's all peaceful and quiet. I must go before dawn breaks. I will come back here. It feels so perfect, and you are such a good man!" Maxx took her hand and kissed it. Lucia sighed.

"Goodbye," Lucia whispered.

"I'll see you tomorrow night! I'll leave the door open."

"Maxx, don't forget, I am just a spirit!" Lucia tore herself away from his hand and left without making a sound.

After the girl left, Maxx lay down in bed. He heard the door and thought she had returned.

"Lucia? You are back?"

"No, young sir, it's Eufrasia! What's wrong? Are you sick? What did the countess do to you?"

"She hasn't done anything to me; I'm just a bit dazed; I talked with her about so many things."

"This being "dazed" is not good! I felt that, too, when I was young. Maybe you're in love."

"Do you think that's possible?"

"If you ask me, I think you've fallen for her, Mr. Maxx. And this is not good. When I met my love, my eyes were shining for him just like your eyes are shining now! He died in the war, and I have never gotten over it. I could not love anyone else. And I don't have children, either."

"Lucia will come here every night. She is waiting for Luis de Luso and their baby. When they come, they will never be apart again. The child stayed with the count, by I don't know what divine law, and they meet by the river for only one week. The baby cried because he wanted to be with both his parents."

"Poor miserable soul!"

"Lucia says that all three of them will be happy now."

"You know, young master, it seemed to me that she was upset when she came downstairs."

"I told her that she had been seen and that everybody in the area knows about her, but come she will anyway, so she told me. Now go and get some sleep. Will you be there with me tomorrow night?"

"Yes, master Maxx, I shall stay in the niche until she calms down. But be careful, child, do not fall for her! She hasn't got eyes for you!"

"I know, that is the only thing holding me back from making any further gesture. And yet, I touched her, I kissed her hand, I held her hand. She was so real, just like the rest of us!"

"Good Lord! I shall say a prayer for you! Now go to sleep and do not think about her!" Eufrasia left the room quietly and went to her own room. The castle was deep in complete silence.

CHAPTER 7

Maxx, his head in a whirl because of the lack of sleep, finally managed to get out of bed. As he went downstairs, he looked for traces of the girl, but could find nothing. Not even a crease where she had sat on the chair. She hadn't left anything behind when she left his room. He slowly went to the basin and started to wash himself, hoping to wake up, but the dark rings around his eyes and the look on his face betrayed his fatigue.

He came downstairs carefully. "She passed by here," he said to himself, and he headed for the breakfast table. He noticed that everyone else was already there, waiting for him.

"Come on, son, I've been waiting for you for five minutes. Your mother wouldn't let me begin without you. But what's got into you? You look as if you had spent the whole night looking at the stars. Don't tell me... Don't tell me: 'someone' visited you..."

"Yes, father, I mean – nobody visited me, it's just that I could not sleep." The women had a sense that there was more to it, but said nothing. But the banker went on:

"Did the Countess try your door handle?"

"Yes, father."

"And did you get scared?"

"A bit, but she persisted, and then I couldn't fall asleep anymore." Maxx sat down at the table, where he was noticeably absent-minded; he dropped the sugar, spilled the tea. He dropped a slice of bread on his trousers. He was clearly ill at ease.

"I think you should come with me to the office today. I believe you'd get back on your feet. This countess and her nonsense! I'll sleep in your room," the banker said.

"No, father, I'm fine."

"Yes... I can see that! I think you are coming with me to Coimbra."

"Leave Maxx alone," his mother's low voice could be heard. "I'll give him a sedative and I'll stay by his side until he falls asleep."

"Did you hear that, Maxx? Your mother will pamper you today. You're off the hook; you don't have to come with me after all. Maybe after this Pentecost week, you'll get back to your old self. Maybe this countess will disappear once and for all!"

"Yes, father."

"Now, let's eat before our food gets cold and I have to leave hungry. If you want to lavish attention on Maxx, go ahead and pamper him until he falls asleep!" Nobody said anything anymore; they all ate their breakfast quietly. After the banker left, Rosa went to talk to Maxx.

"My dear son, could you please come to my room?"

"Yes, mother."

They went upstairs, Maxx following closely behind her. When they reached her room, Rosa asked him directly:

"You opened the door to her, didn't you? Please don't lie to me, I know you without your having to say even a single word. You are dizzy because of her -- not to mention 'in love.' You have to be careful, son, for she is different! We shall be like that at some point, but right now we are different, we are alive!"

"Mother, she is so beautiful! I touched her, and she is not made of air; she is alive, only she is cold and pale."

"So the servants were right!"

"Yes, but don't be afraid. She will leave soon, when her husband and child come to get her. She will leave from here for good. She just wanted to see her house and room. When I fell off the windowsill and broke it, I found her diary underneath. I read it, but it didn't tell me very much."

"I think you're falling for her, my dear."

"I'll be all right, I'll get over that. I'll just be a bit different for a couple of days. I know she does not belong to me, but I can't get her out of my mind so easily."

"Don't you want to have a cup of tea and then get some sleep? I'll stay here by your side."

"Thank you, mother. I really will need your help these next few days, until Count de Luso gets here."

After his tea, Maxx went to sleep in his room with the windows wide open. His mother took a book and sat beside him, watching him. "Poor baby, he'll get over this, too. It will last only a few more days..." Mrs. Rosa sighed and continued reading. The girls came in, too, but their mother waved them away, letting them know that everything was all right. Maxx was sleeping peacefully. A couple of hours later, he woke up refreshed

"My sweetheart, are you all right?"

"Yes, mother. I have one more thing to ask of you, for I really want to work this out on my own. Do not come out at night, promise me! I will tell you everything, every morning after you put me to sleep with your teas." Mrs. Rosa took a deep breath.

"Is that what you want?"

"I feel that it is enough if you are by my side in spirit. I'll get through this somehow."

"That is a heavy promise you are asking of me, but so be it. I trust you."

"Thank you! You are the best mother in the world! I feel stronger with such an ally by my side. I will ask Christian to saddle my horse; I think I will go for a ride."

"That is a good idea. It will chase these thoughts away."

"Christian," he shouted out of the window, "saddle my horse! I am going for a ride."

"Yes, master, right away!"

"I shall be back by lunchtime, do not worry about that, mother."

"Yes, darling, go ahead!"

His mother watched him as he got on his horse and headed for the plain by the river. He rode slowly along the riverbank. "What do I really think I will find? There's nothing here!" Everything around him was pulsing with life. The birds were singing in the willows, one more beautifully than the other; everything was green, alive, colorful, fragrant. The black soil abounded with life, and farther on, he could see the flocks scattered in the fields looking for soft grass. He got off his horse and sat on the river bank.

"How beautiful everything is! It is like a fairytale! And how tranquil the Mondego is! The river doesn't care about anything. It always flows like this, without stopping. How many secrets does it hide, I wonder? But Mondego is silent and stubborn, and it does what it has enjoyed doing for so many centuries."

A little frog jumped into the water when he threw a pebble. "Lucia! You belong to another man! And I will let you be; it's just that I want to see you a few more times. Then I will let go of my pain and become the old me. I shall go with my father to the bank, and that will be that!" He stood up, ready to go back. He had to make it home for lunch, and he was already feeling better. He had in some way come to terms with that love of his. But at home, he felt a certain tension in the ladies of the house, and they would not dare bring the subject up for discussion. They knew it would all be over soon. Eufrasia was a trustworthy partner; she did not say one word. When she was alone with Maxx, she talked to him about courage, about the strength to move on past that impossible love, without denying its existence.

The banker forgot all about it and did not even bring the subject up at dinner. It was clear to him that that was more of a female thing. He didn't tell Maxx to switch rooms; maybe Lucia would be scared away by his ugliness. So he went to his room, pleased with what he had accomplished that day at work, pleased with his business, and content like a child who holds his toy in his arms for a comforting and well deserved sleep.

Maxx went to sleep, too, without locking his door. But at midnight nobody came in through his door. Hearing a short tap at the window, Maxx quickly opened the window. Lucia came in like a breeze.

"I thought that I shouldn't be seen anymore."

"Lucia, I thought you were not coming again! I have very strong feelings for you! Today I took a ride by the river. I felt as if I wanted to find something of you, even if so many years have gone by. Something alive from you!"

"Maxx," she said, "I repeat, I am from another world, and I am waiting for my family! Do not attempt to love a soul without a body! Where I stay is different from where I come to you at night. It's not like on earth. It's just me and my thoughts from that time, from the life I lived. I cannot understand and love a man from another century, from another world. I couldn't possibly! My life stopped then! My soul has been searching for something lost since then, so it is impossible for me to start something new. Do you understand that?"

"I understand that you can't possibly love someone in this present time."

"Exactly! I am just waiting for Luis and my baby, for they belong to that time, my time."

"But what about me?"

"You will find a living girl from your own time. Maybe it will be difficult, but if she loves you, she will help you get through this!" Lucia was obsessed only with her need, her life, cut short in 1650, which she wanted to restore now. Maxx's mind knew that Lucia was right, but love knows no borders, no boundaries.

"I know what you're thinking," Lucia continued, "but I can't offer you anything! Be strong and confident; as I have a fate and a soul mate, so do you – but that has nothing to do with me."

"You are right. What are you going to do now?"

"I shall linger some more and wait. If he doesn't come tonight, I shall keep coming here until he finds me. I think Luis also has a long way to go to get here."

"You loved each other very much..."

"We still love each other, but we are not yet beside each other. I can feel him getting close to me." Silence settled over Maxx's room. Quietness encompassed everything. The boy was simply looking at her. He knew that loving her was impossible, and he was suffering. "I think he is not coming, so I will leave, again by the window. Take care of yourself and my room. I'll come back tomorrow night. Goodbye!"

Lucia climbed on the window sill, and then let herself go. Maxx ran to the window immediately, but he could hear only some steps growing fainter, and notice a light perfume. Lucia's. Lucia didn't have a body anymore. Maxx went downstairs to Eufrasia, in control as much as he could be under the circumstances.

"She didn't come?"

"Yes, she came through the window, and when she left, she jumped into the void, but she no longer had a body. You could hear only her steps, but you could not see her. Luis and her child haven't found her yet. She thinks they are trying hard to reach her. She will keep coming here until they meet."

"Are you more relaxed now, more peaceful?"

"I think so. She has remained with her body and soul in 1650, and she cannot love a man from our times. I have that ability; I can do this, but she can't. She seems to be locked in her time!"

"I'm glad, master, my child, that you are more collected now. You were terrible during breakfast!"

"Mother has figured it all out, she knows! But it's like an exercise of nerves for me, and she lets me be. I know it is an impossible situation, but I shall drink the glass to the bottom. Now let's go to sleep, so we can be rested in the morning. I have an idea and I need to sleep on it. She will not come back until tomorrow night. I think I'm getting used to it. No mortal has the chance to love a being from another time. I think Lucia is someone who is leaving now and is waiting for the coming night in some parallel world. There may be such a thing!"

"I don't know about that, but maybe you're right! Good night."

"Good night."

In the morning, as if he had slept all night long, Maxx came out of his room and went to the kitchen. There he found Eufrasia, who was preparing the bread.

"Good morning! Give me something to eat, because I want to leave today, and fix me some food for the trip, too, for I will come back late."

"What shall I say if they ask about you, master?"

"Tell them I will be back in the evening, and they should not worry about me, but I have to do something that cannot be postponed. If you promise to keep your mouth shut, I will tell you!" Eufrasia quickly agreed, driven by curiosity. "I want to go to Luso, to the crypt of the Count's family. Does this family have any successors? Is the castle still there?"

"Yes, the castle is still there, and there is also a Count de Luso. The castle has always been occupied. It has never been empty. It is beautiful and well managed, well taken care of. The family crypt is in the cemetery. Ask the guard nicely to let you in, and mention my name; we are from the same village."

"Very well, thank you; I'm leaving now."

"Take care, master... you tormented soul..." but Maxx didn't hear those last words.

He went out and got on his horse. The sun had barely risen, and it was wonderful to ride. But the boy didn't notice any of that. The whole family asked about him, but Eufrasia reassured them that when he returned, he would tell them all about it. Everyone should just relax.

"Then let's stay calm," the banker said. Eufrasia didn't tell them that he was going to Luso; she said it only later that day to Mrs. Lieberman, who remained speechless.

"I think that is part of the healing. Last night, she came in through the window, so Mr. Maxx told me."

"We can do nothing but wait," the mistress of the house said, going upstairs to her room.

Maxx rode until he saw the castle on the horizon. "This must be it!" It wasn't hard for him to find the cemetery, but it was closed. An old man, who must have heard him approaching, came out and asked what he wanted.

"You don't seem to be from around here, young man," the guard said.

"I am from Coimbra; I want to see a particular grave. Eufrasia, our cook, told me to remind you that you and she are from the same village."

"Ah, Eufrasia! That is some woman! I'll get the keys right away. I knew her husband. She never wanted to marry again; she loved only once. I would have married her in a second; instead, I am all alone, and so is she. Please, come in! Which grave do you wish to see?"

"The crypt of the Counts de Luso. My father bought the castle of Count de Sousa y Monterro, and we now live there. I want to see the grave of Lucia de Luso!"

"Oh, God, that is the girl who drowned, the girl who haunted the river year after year. Everybody knows the story. Her father died at her funeral, for he felt guilty. He rushed to her grave and then simply remained there, dead. He is buried at your castle, not here. A great curse occurred then. Here is the grave. It is next to her husband Luis."

"These are well tended graves."

"Yes, there are always some servants from the castle who come over and clean away the weeds. They take care of all the dead, but especially these two."

"The statues on the grave are so old," Maxx noticed.

"Yes, well, they date back to those times. They clean them, but the blackness of time does not wash away. I also come by from time to time; I like this angel with his bent wings, and the Madonna with the child. They say that the Countess was carrying a child. Her brother married Luis's sister. They overcame that scandal, and together, they forgave and forgot."

"It's wonderful here, it is so peaceful! You are surrounded by so many dead people. Doesn't that affect you? Aren't you afraid of them?"

"Me?" The old man smiled wordlessly. "Not at all! The dead won't hurt you; only the living do that. Remember this."

"I have to go now; here is a penny for your trouble, and many thanks!"

"Don't mention it, son, and do come back; there are other beautiful graves to see, not just this one."

"Goodbye!"

"Have a safe trip, young man!"

Maxx, after eating what Eufrasia had packed for him, got on his horse and slowly rode back home. The sun had gone behind the clouds, a sign that there might be rain, which was good for the soil. When he arrived home, everybody was waiting for him full of questions, but he talked only to his mother.

"I saw her grave; she is indeed Countess de Luso. She can belong only to Luis de Luso. There is an angel on her grave and a Madonna with her baby. The de Luso castle is still occupied by the de Luso counts. Their crypt is very well taken care of. Don't be angry with me, dear mother, but these confirmations help me."

"I understand, sweetheart; soon, it will all be over, I can feel it. You will find your peace."

"I feel that, too. One or two more days, and she will be gone. Luis will find her. Lucia tells me that she can feel it, she can feel him coming closer and closer, with every night that goes by."

"Will you still see her until that moment comes?"

"Yes, mother, she comes to her room, not mine. Relax, I will get over this."

"I know that. You are strong, but you are also sensitive, just like me."

"Sometimes it's good to be sensitive. It doesn't always spoil things. Where is father?"

"He's in the library; I told him that you are sleeping, for you left early this morning."

"Thank you for the lie," Maxx chuckled. "I feel like eating something, I'm going to see if Eufrasia can make me something to eat."

"Go, darling; if I see your father, I'll tell him you woke up."

"Please tell the girls to forgive me for not paying attention to them now. Soon, it will be different."

"Relax, son. They understand you, too; they are not frightened anymore. They are also your confidantes. Your father has no idea what you are up to, but after this episode, you will have to go with him to the office. You won't be able to avoid that any longer."

"I will!"

Eufrasia gave him something to eat while Maxx told her about her old admirer. She laughed, holding her hands to her chest.

"What a man! He hasn't forgotten me to this day!"

That night, Lucia again came through the window. But the rain hadn't touched her. She was not wet at all.

"No one would stay outside. Nobody saw me."

"I thought you wouldn't come tonight because of the rain."

"Nothing touches me, Maxx. And I've told you before that I must attain my goal. Luis will come, I can feel it."

"Today I went to Luso, to your grave. It is very well tended. There is an angel with bent wings there; it is very beautiful!"

"I know about the statues and I also know about your visit there. But why did you go? There's nothing there! My body belongs to Mother Earth, and my soul belongs to Father Heaven. That is why you must not love me. You are not from where I come from. But my husband is. He and I match. He must be coming; I can feel him closer and closer. I can feel his shortness of breath; he comes from far away, and he is taking care of our son. The impatience is burning me inside; my soul is like a burning pyre. I

104

think that I will soon put out my fire! Come, Luis, come!" Lucia said, closing her eyes....

CHAPTER 8

Maxx could not fall asleep for quite a long time after Lucia left. He was suffering terribly because she didn't return his feelings. In his soul, he knew she was right, for they were different beings; even so, his heart was aching. He couldn't show her his feelings anymore; he spoke in vain, as one would talk to a flower pot. She had only one goal, and that was to wait for Luis. Maxx remembered the graves in Luso. They were joined, bound together in marriage. They belonged to each other. "Maybe I should look for a girl of my own, just as she said. One from my own century, one who is alive...." He closed his eyes and finally fell asleep with the window open. In the morning, after breakfast, Maxx wanted to talk to his mother. She took him by the hand and led him to her room.

"My darling, how pale you are!"

"Yes, mother. She came again last night. She said the strangest things. Did you know that yesterday I went to see their graves? She said to me: 'Why did you go there? There's nothing in that ground!'"

"Maybe she is right; she knows more than we all do, for she's seen the other world, too. But you must get some rest; your father has left, and I will sit here with you as I have been doing. I'm thinking that maybe I should talk to your father; I think it would be appropriate for you to have a girlfriend. He would know which of his friends has a daughter suited to you and your sensitivity, one who would understand you and help you get over all of this. Would you be willing to try that?"

"Yes, mother. After Lucia leaves. I also thought it would be a good idea to choose someone from my century!"

"And someone who is alive, my beloved child! I'm glad that you agree. Anyway Lucia will come back once or twice more, at the most. The Pentecost is coming to its end, and so is the curse of that medicine man. Sweetheart, you have to confront this only one or two more times! I know about Eufrasia, too. I talked to her and she told me everything. Our problem now is the village. If only you could imagine how the village people talk! I'm afraid they will lurk about by the castle doors or hit

106

someone in the head, to kill the fiend! Those two servants did us a lot of harm, but we can't dismiss them, because they have families and they could denounce us. They are hard-working, I can't deny that, but they know that the girl comes to your room every night. Eufrasia heard them talk. Fortunately, Eufrasia is helping us. She told them that these holy days would be over soon, and that any ghost will go away after that. They are a bit less concerned, also, because she enters only your room. They say they saw her come in through the window one night, and they watched until she left. And they also say that after she climbed on the windowsill to leave, they didn't see her anymore, but only heard the rustle of her dress. They saw some traces in the fine sand on the reception platform. Eufrasia had them both pray for you, so that you will have the strength to endure all of this. And I believe that settled them down. They're thinking of saying a prayer, a joint prayer uttered by everyone in the village. But I am still afraid!"

"You don't have to worry, dear mother! Let them say the prayer – maybe it will help me! I think I will go and thank them. They believe in the same God. I don't think there are several Gods out there, but He is revealed to each nation so that He is understood. Look, I'll go find them and talk to them. You wait for me. I'll come back soon to get some sleep. You'll see, I'll help you find your peace, too."

Maxx came downstairs as his sisters were going upstairs. He kissed them both and told them he loved them both very much. Then he went out through the back door. He looked for the two servants and found them working on one of the benches in the park. He stopped in front of them and said:

"Good morning!"

They stood up and answered: "Good morning, Mr. Maxx! What can we do for you?"

"First, I want to thank you for your kindness. I've heard that you are saying a prayer for me. I'm begging you to! I will draw strength from you! I think that Lucia will still come once or twice more, but this is hard for me. Please say whatever prayer you want, and say it from your hearts. It doesn't matter what religion each of us has! Could you do this tonight and tomorrow night? But without my father learning about it! He doesn't believe in this, he thinks this is all nonsense; he is very pragmatic, and only his bank and the money matter to him."

"Dear God, young sir, do you really want us to do this?"

"I'm not asking you, I'm begging you to do it! Go together some place and pray for me. These days haven't been easy for me, but I'll get back on my feet after she leaves. She will soon go away; she already senses that Luis and their baby are getting close. Can you promise me this?"

"Yes, with all our heart! We will finish mending this bench and then we will go to the village."

"And I am going to get some sleep; I am exhausted."

"Do not worry, master, we are with you! We weren't expecting you to ask this of us. We should be the ones thanking you. We'll gather everyone together tonight on the river bank. Sleep well, master; we'll all pray hard for her to go away!"

"Thank you once again; I'm going now to get some sleep."

The servants bowed and continued working to finish quickly what they had to do, for they had a mission to accomplish. Maxx went back to his room, and told his mother that they would all gather that night and the next night to join in prayer on the river bank. He felt he had put their fears to rest.

"You are a true diplomat, my son; now get some sleep while I read."

Maxx fell asleep immediately, confident that everything would soon be all right, and his unfortunate love would blow away with the wind, where it had all come from in the first place.

That evening, the two servants gathered the whole village to pray together. Maxx came near them unobtrusively and sat beside his servants. He listened to their prayers without saying a word. However, he noticed their passion. It didn't last long, only half an hour, but it was wonderful. Then Maxx stood up and spoke to the group:

"Thank you, my friends, you are helping me very much! I shall come back tomorrow night!"

The people gathered there were glad, for they were doing a good deed and they knew it was appreciated. Then the gathering dispersed, and everyone said "We will come again tomorrow." Maxx left with his servants.

"How did you manage to get them all here?"

"These are kind and warm-hearted people, master, and you are a good man. You deserve our prayers for you even if our religion is different. We are all human."

"Yes, you are right! You are wise."

"Night is drawing near; let us hope that our prayers will help you."

"They will; I can feel it."

After dinner, he went upstairs to his room. He was sitting and thinking to himself, "I love you, Lucia, but I shall love you no more; I shall suffer, but I shall forget you!" When the monastery clock struck midnight, Lucia appeared in his room again, but this time she entered through the door.

"Hello, Maxx, how are you?"

"I was waiting for you, my sweetheart, darling one!"

"Maxx, please! You must understand this, I cannot be yours!"

"I know that. You've said it a thousand times! Don't say it anymore! I will leave you behind, forget you, but I need some time. Come sit next to me, for just a little while. Let me hold your hand." Lucia sighed and put her hand in his.

"Your love cannot touch me, and yet, every time I come here, I feel a deep restlessness, a pain I cannot explain. I wonder if it would be better for me not to come anymore. I can think only of my husband; I cannot possibly be thinking of some other man!"

"Lucia, when you leave from here at night, do you forget about me or am I still there in your memory?"

"I have you in my mind, and that is not good. I am grateful that Luis is getting near. I can hear the baby now, too, and I think we shall soon be together. I shall be happy again, after all this time!"

"Will you still come to your room?"

"Yes, I have to, but do you know something? When I first came in here, I felt good; it felt like home. Now I feel out of place, like a stranger. This room has a different owner now – you! The castle has a new master, your father! I think I'm beginning to break free from this place. You must forget me. But wait! I hear something! Luis is talking to me, saying "tomorrow, tomorrow!" Can you hear it too?"

"No, I can't hear anything," Maxx said, letting go of Lucia's hand.

"Don't be upset!

"I'm not upset. It's just that none of this is easy for me."

"Let me tell you what "MY room" was like back then," Lucia said, changing the subject. "It had a beautiful bed, with pink curtains. I had a sofa with two chairs where sometimes I would have a cup of tea or something to eat. My dresser was nice and full of perfumed envelopes. I had flowers all over the place, an icon that is no longer there, and a painting. My father had a painter come to our castle when I was sixteen, to paint my portrait. The current Count de Sousa had this painting now. My letters to Luis were hidden under the matting of the picture frame. I wanted to take it when I came here, but the Count had gotten here first. What I loved most was my orange canary. I was a bit absent-minded, and I would often forget to close the door to its cage, but it never flew away. It was quite well-trained. I also had some shelves with my favorite books. From here, I first saw Luis. My brother and he were coming back from the

University in Lisbon. They were traveling in the de Luso family carriage. When our eyes met, I felt a throbbing in my heart. Later, Luis confessed to me that he felt the same way about me. He didn't stay too long that evening. He was tired and wanted to get home. His family was waiting for him. But later, we met by the river. But what importance does that have now? – There was also a thick carpet in the room. Now it is colder, and it looks like a man's room. Everything is decorated in a different style, less glamorous. I see that the chandelier is no longer there either!"

"They are all under cover in the attic. Would you like me to restore it the way it was before?"

"No, I will be leaving anyway. Luis told me tomorrow night. I am waiting for him to come here."

"Do you know that the people said a prayer tonight, a joint prayer, on the bank of the Mondego river?"

"Yes, I know, I saw it all! These are good people, like you, but those prayers troubled me terribly. A prayer said by so many people can crush things. Such prayer has the power of a cannon. But I must hear it tomorrow as well. Then I will leave and never return! You must forget about me, Maxx. There are so many beautiful girls in the world. I must go now; I think I will go out through the window. I don't know why, but I felt people looking at me when I came up the stairs."

"Lucia, they saw you at the window as well. I will wait for you tomorrow for the last time!"

But the girl had vanished into the night.

CHAPTER 9

"For the last time!" Maxx said again. "After that, I shall never see her again. It's better this way; I shall prevail! I don't think I can stay here tonight! I'm going to mother's room. She always makes me feel better." He knocked at her door and whispered: "Mother!" Mrs. Rosa opened her door at once.

"Let me sleep in here, mother! I can't sleep in there tonight! Tomorrow, Lucia's leaving for good. Her mind really is somewhere else. I shall get over this somehow. After this, I shall go with my father to the bank, and I shall finish my studies. It's something I must do!"

The door opened and the two sisters came in and took their brother into their arms.

"Maxx, be strong; hold on just one more night! We promise you that we will introduce you to an ideal girl!" Maxx started laughing.

"My sisters, you are already making me feel better."

"Mother, tonight we are all going to sleep in your room."

"And I am so glad, my dear children! We must help Maxx any way we can."

"Do you all know that Lucia was at the vigil by the river last night? She said that all that praying hurt her, but she will come again tonight, the last night of Pentecost! Something compels her to be there. She says that a great sorrow encompasses her when people pray, so many people together."

"Maxx, she is nothing but an apparition! Can't you see that she can't stand the dawn? She is beautiful, she is elusive, but she is still just a ghost! She can't stand the prayers! And then think about it; she died without a candle at her head. They held only the religious wedding service and the funeral service, but no Catholic Mass before her burial and after her death. Probably that is why the curse remained, because she did not take communion, and she didn't confess, either. She didn't say goodbye to her relatives! Nothing of this! That is why she is walking around the castle," Miriam said. "She is trying to be understood, or who knows what else! She was born here; back then there were no hospitals," Miriam went on.

"I think so, too," Anna said. "A ghost cannot bear to listen to prayers, but something makes her come to the vigil; maybe that is how she will be freed of all that. Who knows? Only God above us!"

"Have courage, my son! This is the last night! Now we should get some rest. You can all stay here. I'll be happiest if we do that. If only my husband understood this!" Mrs. Rosa sniffed. "You, Maxx, you sleep on the couch, and the three of us in bed. There's plenty of room for everybody."

"And, look," Anna said, "I locked the door. Let's go to sleep; we will need our energy." The candle burned down, and everybody tried to find a "nest" for a good night's sleep.

Towards the morning, they all went to their own rooms so that no one would know about their spending the night with their mother. They promised each other they would do the same the next night, the last night. Nothing unusual happened during the day. Maxx went to the park with his sisters; they walked, they ate, and then they rested, waiting for the evening to settle in. His sisters decided to go to the vigil as well.

"If they accepted you, then we'll go, too! We want to be there by your side!"

Later that day, Maxx went downstairs to the kitchen. Eufrasia and the other servants were eating.

"Master, is there something that you need?"

"Well, first of all, enjoy your meal; I didn't know I would find you eating. I just came to tell you that tonight she will come for the last time. Luis let her know that he would come with their child. Tonight, my sisters will join me by the river; they want to be there at my side. I trust that will not be a problem, will it?"

"No problem at all, my boy," Eufrasia replied. "How could that be a problem? We are all humans. The Inquisition is long gone now, isn't that so, fellows?

"That is true," they replied.

"Lucia became very distressed because of the prayers last night. But somebody or something compels her to stay there and listen. She can't leave and she can't stop the feeling. She said there were too many of us praying and that she has no choice but to listen. She didn't tell me what it is that forces her to listen, though."

"Master, she died without a candle, and she didn't die naturally. She took her own life there in the river. Probably she feels some pain; maybe she feels the power of the river they jumped into. We cannot

112

possibly know what she feels. She was a Christian. It is such a pity and a sin to take your own life! The young ladies, your sisters, can come, too. There is no problem!"

"I have suffered terribly," Maxx said, "and I am eager to pray again tonight. There is strength in our great numbers. I believe that Lucia sees a vision of how she jumped into the river back then. It hurts her, I suppose. Now I'll let you finish your meal. I have bothered you enough!"

"You haven't bothered us at all, master."

After Maxx left, the servants said that the Liebermans were nice people, and they wondered how they had come to have this trouble. They might be Jewish, but the villagers loved them, for they were good people.

"This night will be over sometime. I won't even go to sleep. I shall watch and see her leave with her family," Eufrasia said.

"My God, you are right! We won't go to sleep either! Tomorrow morning, you'll make some strong coffee, and we shall make it through the day. It is a weekend, so it will not be that hard!"

On their way to the Mondego river, as it was getting dark, Maxx and his sisters – whom their father allowed to accompany him, although he himself was quite confused and astonished – walked to the river. Maxx told himself, who knows for how many times, that he must forget Lucia, let her go, and move on with his life. Seeing the other people fortified his self-control, and he began to feel that he could leave all this behind him and look to the future. The prayers calmed him and gave him strength.

As he knelt, he heard moans coming from the river. He looked around, curious to see if the others heard what he did. One by one, without interrupting their prayer, people turned their head towards the Mondego. "Yes! They can all hear that! Lucia is there, in the river – actually her spirit is. It is from there that she will come tonight. But isn't Luis also in the river? Maybe he is farther away," Maxx said to himself. At the end of the prayer, people threw basil into the water: "Be gone, be gone from here!" they shouted. Then they shook hands, one by one, with Maxx and left to return to their homes, torches in their hands.

"Thank you!" That's all that Maxx could say; he led his sisters back to the castle.

"Maxx, did you hear the groaning coming from the water? There was so much pain in that! She will leave for certain! One more night of praying will overcome her!" The girls were talking, both at the same time, sharing their feelings with each other.

"And those weeds thrown into the water! I do hope," Miriam went on, "that this will come to an end. I for one am composed now. I'm thinking about father and how he let us leave the house late at night, without eating anything."

"Well, he had an intimate dinner with mother instead," Anna laughed.

"Yes, you are right, Anna!

The banker was indeed amazed, but not afraid. He felt there was something to all of this, but he wasn't interested enough to find out what it was. Maybe later – but what was certain was that it had all started with the Countess de Luso. His wife was eating without saying a word, and the servants were also completely quiet. "Hmm, some dinner! I think I'll go to bed. I'll find out everything tomorrow." He stood up from the table, saying he was going to his room. He was sleepy. Then he saw his children entering the yard. "Excellent! Now I can truly sleep peacefully! They can eat whatever is left from dinner; it is already cold now."

That night, no one slept except for Mr. Lieberman. It seemed they were all waiting for something. They wanted to see for themselves, to be present during that last night the countess would spend in her family's castle. Everyone was sitting in the kitchen. Eufrasia was ruling in her own yard. Everybody wanted to see Luis as well.

Finally, Maxx said goodnight to the ladies of the family and went to his room. Then they all went to Mrs. Rosa's room. They couldn't sleep. They were wide awake, waiting for Lucia's and Maxx's deliverance. At midnight, people were hiding in the dark corners of the front stairs, from where the main stairs ascended, people who had set their minds on seeing the countess. They had gathered calmly and unobtrusively, and had taken their places in silence. Eufrasia had her usual spot in the library niche.

Suddenly, when the monastery bell stopped, Lucia came in sadly through the door. She was so tired, as if she had been carrying millstones. Her lovely white dress emphasized her paleness even more. She slowly started climbing every step of the staircase, but it appeared her feet weren't listening to her anymore.

She heard a noise, maybe some careless servant; she turned around, but then continued to climb up the whole stairs. She realized that she had been seen and somehow accepted. She was a spirit. She made it up the stairs and she was exhausted. Then she continued her trip to her room, which was her goal. She opened the door, and then gently closed it. Maxx was there to catch her as she fell.

"What are you doing? Leave me alone! I'm waiting for my husband and baby. Those prayers of yours made me terribly tired!"

"We all heard you sighing in the Mondego," Maxx said, putting her down in an armchair.

114

"I must follow my destiny, Maxx! You have your own destiny, so mind your own self! You are troubling me, and just now you took me in your arms!"

"You are exhausted, and I helped you!"

"You love me; you did not help me! I can hardly wait to get out of here! Nothing belongs to me anymore! My mother has been dead for a long, long time. Others will always and forever own this castle. When I got upstairs, I felt eyes watching me. And, dear God, this used to be my house, my home, my room, my park, my flowers! What am I now? A ghost! I can hear Luis, closer and closer; he's telling me that he's coming soon. I'm waiting for you, my love! Take me away from this world! Let's go there where it is so quiet!"

Maxx looked at her, astounded, and did not make a sound. He remembered the girl's diary. He got up on his feet and gave it to her.

"This surely belongs to you!"

"Ah, the diary! I hid it there where I was sure that no one would ever find it. I didn't think that anything from here would ever belong to anyone other than the Counts de Sousa y Monterro. How proud they were! But you had to fall off the windowsill and discover it all!"

"Not quite all of it. I don't have the painting. The current count has it. You said that there were letters inside its frame."

"Ha ha ha ha ha!" Lucia started laughing, but it was an ugly laugh which did not match her nature, a laugh from another world, another voice, a strange one. "One night I went to Coimbra, after I left from here. I visited the count. I saw his happy children, and his wife, sleeping. I took the painting and looked for the letters. They were all there. I put them in fire, in the count's fireplace. Then I put the painting back and left."

Dawn was drawing near. She stood suddenly and threw the diary into the fire. "This doesn't belong to you – or me either!" Flames consumed every page, until the diary had burned up completely. "That is over! You people from the future don't have to interfere anymore in my family's past!"

"Lucia," Maxx said, in a restrained voice.

"Leave me alone! I can hear Luis; he is getting closer and closer! Soon, he will be here. He will set me free! The curse will be undone; I can feel this weight on my heart lifted up, this sepulcher stone that has crushed me for so long! Luis, Luis, my love, come! Come faster! I am suffocating in this room! God, all this fatigue! Those senseless prayers pierced my heart with a thousand arrows! I hate you all! Luis, Luis, where are you?" Suddenly, silence set in the room. "Listen! I can hear his steps nearby! He will call me soon!" Abruptly, Lucia stood up. "He is calling me! I'm

115

coming, my baby, I'm coming; I'm going downstairs right away! The chains of the curse are finally broken!"

Her energy apparently restored, Lucia hurried out of the room and rushed down the stairs without casting a single glance at Maxx. The young man waited for her at the window. A little distance from the door, two silhouettes became more and more clear. One large silhouette was holding a small one by the hand. The two went in through the door and waited for Lucia. Then the man looked up and saw Maxx. The child didn't notice any of that. His icy glitter froze Maxx. He belonged to Lucia's world, as Maxx understood. Lucia had to take what was rightly hers. She came out of the castle and they ran toward one another. They embraced and kissed. Lucia took the baby into her arms; she looked at him lovingly, and then kissed him a thousand times.

"Mother, mother!" the little boy cried joyously.

"Yes, my beloved ones, we will never be apart ever again, not ever! The curse has been undone! Do you feel that, Luis?"

"Yes, my darling, we finally belong one to another!"

"The castle belongs now to someone else. It has been sold, and the current Count de Sousa now lives in a palace in the center of Coimbra."

"Let's go, Lucia, it is late," Luis said.

Before turning around, Luis bowed to Maxx, who bowed in return. Lucia just glanced up; to her, nothing else mattered. She was passionately kissing her child, and he was no longer crying, but happy, for they were together again. All three of them turned around and went through the gate. Maxx watched them, their shadows fading farther and farther away. At one point, one of the shadows turned around. It was Lucia. She climbed onto the gate and pulled down the family coat of arms. The two delicate, yet merciless aigrettes would no longer guard the castle. Someone else was the owner now. Then she waved goodbye and vanished from sight into the darkness, together with her family at last.

When he came back to his senses, Maxx realized that warm tears were running down his cheeks. He ran out of his room to his mother.

"Mother," he whispered through his tears, closing his eyes. "She's gone! Luis came for her, and their little son was there, too. The Count de Luso greeted me, mother, and then he bowed and left. And, mother, Lucia pulled their coat of arms with aigrettes from the gate and took it with her. She waved goodbye. She was happy. She said that the Counts de Sousa were no longer the masters here. The curse is gone. And along with it, I came to understand and accept all this. Luis is what Lucia needs, he is her world."

"Yes, my dear, Lucia has known that for two hundred years!"

116

"I am so happy for her! I also want a girl like that, as devoted and loving as she was. When I saw Count de Luso, my pain went away."

"Thank God you said that! You are truly cured now!"

"I think I need to get some rest, but I will go to MY room!"

"Go, son, and face reality! You are the present and the future! You are life!"

Maxx closed the door to his room and slept in his own bed like a new-born child, for he had been set free. A few days later, the banker noticed the absence of the coat of arms on the door.

"Lucia took that when her husband came and took her into their world, which is different from ours," Maxx explained.

"Oh... so then it was not a lie?"

"No, it was not!"

"And you... were you in love in her? Was she beautiful?"

"If I used to have feelings for her, I resigned myself to the truth and I shall forget about it. She was from another place, and she remained in her time, around 1650. She came here every night. She told me what her room had been like; she told me also about her brother, about Luis, about their baby, and her former life. Now the story is over, and you have to put something else on the gate instead of that coat of arms."

Shortly after that discussion, one could see engraved on the castle door: "David Lieberman and Family." At last, it belonged to them only!

CHAPTER 10

Silence spread her wings over the valley of the Mondego River. The Liebermans had been completely assimilated into the community since they had attended the prayer vigils. They were considered locals, even if they had a different religion. Maxx decided to continue his studies in Aveiro. He wanted to specialize in the field of economics, more precisely in learning everything he could about banks and all that was related to this complicated business. He thought that in so doing, he would kill two birds with one stone – first, he would study and learn in order to succeed at work in his father's bank, and more important, he would leave Coimbra. He would put that episode in his life behind him. He would come home only on holidays or when he didn't have to attend classes. He was living in an apartment above the branch of his father's bank and he was helping out there as much as he could. In fact, he was doing more learning than creating or producing anything. He still had much to learn before he got to the point of managing others or having ideas. His father was pleased that Maxx accepted living at the bank, "one less expenditure and more deference among his employees." Mr. Lieberman loved money, and one could easily see that in whatever he was doing, whatever his actions or thoughts.

At home at the castle, at Maxx's request, his mother moved his furniture into another room where it was quieter and more conducive to studying. The windows faced the back of the castle, toward the park. Maxx was no longer interested in being a lookout; he just wanted peace. After moving Maxx's things, Lucia's furniture was brought down from the attic. Maxx knew about it from her since the night he opened the door for her. They also found a cage in the attic. Everything looked just as it did in 1650. Another world. The boy decided to lock that room and clean it only once a week.

The Chancellor of the University in Aveiro was a good friend of his father's, with whom he had been doing business for a long time; thus, Maxx was welcome at his house, if he wanted to visit. The Chancellor was glad that he had a student from his one of his friends' children. One evening when he was taking a walk in the center of the city, he called to Maxx, to invite him to their house.

"Good evening, young man; you know me, I am the chancellor of the University; your father is a good friend of mine, so I would like to invite you to come to our house for dinner on Saturday night. I'm not saying you will have fun, but you will get the chance to get out of this hollow above your bank. What do you say?"

"This is a real honor for me, Mr. Zuzarte! Sometimes I do get bored here, for I deal only with school and the bank, every single day."

"Then I won't detain you any longer. I'll be waiting for you. Have a good evening, young man, and I'll see you on Saturday night!"

Mr. Zuzarte told his wife afterwards, "If he could notice Ruth, maybe they wouldn't be so wrapped up in books, either of them."

"You are right, darling. It's worth a try," Mrs. Zuzarte agreed, delighted by his idea.

Maxx was glad, for sometimes he really didn't have anything to do. One should not miss an opportunity like that. He was already thinking about what he should wear and how he should conduct himself; he admitted to himself that he hadn't gone out and socialized much, so he was quite nervous. "Well, there's a first time for everything," he said, smiling. "Wait until mother finds out about this! She will think I am grown up. My goodness! Why would such an important man bother with me?"

On Saturday night, he looked for the street in question and managed to find the right house. It was stately and imposing, just like the reputation of the man living in it. He rang the doorbell, and a butler came to open the door for him.

"Good evening! I am Maxx Lieberman, and I have an invitation from the owner and lady of this house!"

"Good evening, Mr. Lieberman," the servant said, bowing. "I believe you are waited for in the parlor. This way, please!" Maxx went upstairs and entered a hallway. The servant turned a corner into a corridor and opened a door, next to which a huge vase of flowers was placed.

"Mr. Lieberman!" The servant announced the guest, bowed, and closed the door behind Maxx.

"Good evening, Maxx," the chancellor said, laughing. "A bit confused, are you? No worries, we'll take care of you. In his last letter, your father wrote that I should not let you get bored, and that we should all keep you company."

"You mean pamper him, father?" A very pleasant feminine voice could be heard. "Are you willing to be Maxx's 'hen'?" Mr. Zuzarte replied in mock exasperation. But in truth, he was glad.

"Let me introduce my daughter Ruth! She is a very unusual young lady, very witty, but you will see that yourself. You will sit next to her at the table. Ruth is not our only child; she has a sister who is already married, even though she is younger."

"Father, love doesn't come upon command!"

"Naturally, my philosopher daughter! You already know my wife, so I won't introduce her," Mr. Zuzarte added, smiling.

"If I had known you have such a beautiful daughter, I would have brought flowers, Mr. Zuzarte."

"Better not, Maxx, for I would have been very jealous," the lady of the house said, laughing.

"Well, well, some discussion!" The beautiful Ruth pretended to be miffed, though she was laughing. "And look how we are keeping him standing," she added. "Come, take a seat next to me, on this couch. This is an informal dinner, so you must relax. Father doesn't eat people except during reunions with his students; at home, he only eats meat."

Maxx followed respectfully and sat down on the couch next to Ruth. "How the banker would love to see this! I shall write and tell him about it, which will delight him!" Mr. Zuzarte said, visibly satisfied with the visit of banker Lieberman's son.

"My parents are already calling me a spinster, and I am only twenty years old! And only because my sister is eighteen, and she is already married and expecting. Do you think I'm old?"

"You are not old, Ruth. I am almost twenty-five!"

"That doesn't matter for a man. You see, when it comes to men, you are not labeled 'old,' but 'mature,' 'grown-up' or something like that."

"Ruth, you're driving Maxx crazy," the lady of the house declared. "Do you like it in Aveiro?" she then asked.

"Yes, I like these canals and these colorful boats very much. I admire them, it's just that I have never gone out in one of them so far. I don't really have much time. My father makes me study most of the time so that I will be able, one day, to replace him and take over the business."

"And so he should," the chancellor said. "Your father has created something great, something outstanding, and you must carry it on."

Another servant came in, and bowing, announced that dinner was served, so everyone was invited to the table.

"All right, then, let's go into the dining room," Mrs. Zuzarte said. You'll love it here in our house, Maxx!"

"And you will eat well," Ruth burst out laughing.

"Oh, yes, I can guarantee that," Mr. Zuzarte said, smiling proudly.

Maxx smiled and thought to himself, "What an amusing family! I cannot possibly imagine how he can be so severe at school. He's transforming like a chameleon! And their house is so beautiful! And Ruth is so witty! Maybe we'll see each other again in the city, who knows?"

The meal was indeed a feast, but also joyful, and Maxx truly felt wonderful. After dinner, Ruth asked if he would like her to play something for him at the piano, and he thought about Miriam and told them that his sister played the piano quite well. He also added that his father also had two girls to marry off, and then everybody burst out laughing.

"Dear Maxx, a walk after dinner will do us good. Our park is in fact just an enlarged garden, but it's worth seeing it. It doesn't compare to your castle park, but it's quite pleasing."

"Come with me, I'll show it to you," Ruth said enthusiastically. They both went outside happily and walked slowly down the path.

"It's quite lovely, though a bit mysterious, for some reason," Maxx said. "Doesn't it bother you that your parents are pressing you to get married?"

"No, not at all. They both mean well! I don't have a fiancé, but I did once. You see, I've come to know things about him that I didn't like anymore. And I have not had a suitor since then. In fact, it's been only six months. What about you?"

"I have never been engaged. I have had other interests and concerns," Maxx replied.

"That means you have never been in love?"

"That means I have never been engaged, not 'never been in love'!"

"Oh, I'm sorry. It must have hurt so much, and I am a heartless pest, twisting the knife into your wound!"

"It is true that it still hurts," Maxx emphasized the last word, "but life goes on. There must be someone out there for me, too, and I hope that person will show up before I turn too 'mature'."

"Ha ha, you can tell when someone is really joking, and you don't get upset over a joke!"

"But I am spoiled; my mother and my sisters do it all the time when I am at home."

"Spoiled, I am too, thank God!"

"I would like to see you again, as friends," Maxx emphasized, "and when I am home, to write to each other. What do you say to that?"

"That is a good idea, I agree. Now, let's go back inside; it's really dark."

"Oh, and I must go, even if tomorrow is Sunday, I have a lot of things to do!"

"You will come to visit us again, won't you?"

"Yes, of course, if your father invites me to your house again."

That was the beginning of a beautiful and close friendship between the two of them. When Maxx was in Coimbra, they would describe to each other all of their activities. He told her about their park and the river, then asked if she would like to come to visit them at his house someday. He told her about Miriam and Anna, who were by then engaged to be married and who had decided on a whim to have their weddings on the same day. Maxx was already thinking about the double celebration they would have. The girls wanted to be married in the park in front of a magnificent altar, as magnificent as the park itself, and their father already had a headache over that, but his luck was that one would move to Porto, and the other, to Lisbon. Thus he will remain alone. So another migraine for banker Lieberman. When he came back to Aveiro, Maxx took the Zuzartes invitations to his sisters' weddings at the castle.

"My father asks your presence at the weddings from the bottom of his heart. He won't take 'no' for an answer."

"We will certainly be there, dear sir," Mr. Zuzarte replied.

"You are most welcome to stay at our castle for a short vacation after the weddings, if you would like to."

"I would," Ruth said, "and because I am spoiled, my parents will agree, won't they?"

"I suppose we could do that, Ruth," her mother said, "if that's what you want..."

Everyone had an enjoyable time and took advantage of that opportunity to travel, but especially to visit the Liebermans.

"If my ladies want to do that, why would I say no to spending some time with your father," Mr. Zuzarte answered. "We will be there, Maxx, and we will bring wedding presents for the girls."

"Thank you, Sir!"

Time passed, and the friendship between the two became closer and closer, but Maxx remained reserved about his love for Lucia. He would not confess it to Ruth, not just yet. She could hardly wait to go to Coimbra. A castle is always a fairytale place, and this castle also has a prince. "Will my prince be charming?" the girl wondered, sighing. "I think there is a lot weighing on his soul, but I have all the time in the world, and I will wait for him. I'm in no hurry. I think I love him! Oh, my God, that is frightening! I wonder what his feelings are. We only write to each other and that's all? I hope not!"

July came and the wedding drew closer. Ruth became impatient, but she kept telling herself: "I will soon see Maxx!" The trip was lovely. She didn't remember ever traveling so far before. She looked at the vineyards, the hills, the sun-scorched plains; how wonderful nature was! When they arrived at their destination, Maxx helped her down from the carriage and lightly kissed her on her cheek.

"Welcome," he whispered. "I've been looking forward to seeing you again! Let me show you your room."

"What, Maxx, are you taking the girl away? Aren't you going to introduce her?" the banker teased with a wink. He was particularly elated.

"My dear family, this is Miss Ruth Zuzarte, and I will show her to her room now!" Miriam and Anna made a comment, laughing:

"That's an awfully short introduction, but we'll make do with it, brother!"

"Thank you so very much for your tolerance and understanding!"

Maxx and Ruth entered the castle, to the delight and happiness of both families, who were then imagining a third marriage on the horizon. Miriam even said that they should keep the improvised altar, for who knows what the coming days will bring.

The weddings were lovely, and the idea of having a wedding under the blue sky, in open air was brilliant. The girls left with their husbands, and the castle was once again peaceful and quiet. The Zuzartes stayed one more week, a week full of events, actually, for everybody. Maxx and Ruth walked hand in hand on the riverbank, away from the public eye, and he would sometimes dare to caress her cheek or kiss her hand.

"Ruth, my dear, I would like to make you happy, but I am afraid I might fail! I don't want you to be disappointed!"

"You will never disappoint me! You are wonderful!"

"Ruth, oh Ruth," Maxx said, stopping her and taking her into his arms, "I wish this moment would never end!"

"So do I, but we shall be leaving soon. I will be waiting for your letters, impatiently."

"And I will be waiting for your letters, my sweetheart!"

The departure was painful for everyone. The guests had been well received at the castle, and the vacation came to an end too soon. Ruth waved her handkerchief until she was too tired, crying inconsolably.

"I love him, mother," she said, throwing herself into her mother's arms.

Meanwhile, Mrs. Lieberman was convinced in her heart that something was happening, but she kept silent, waiting for Maxx to confess to her.

"Mother, I think I love her, but I am afraid. I think this is all happening too fast, and maybe I have not gotten over Lucia yet."

"Be patient; the Lord will give you strength and will guide you, and, if she loves you, too, she will wait for you. In a few months, you will finish school, and you will see each other again between now and then. You will come back here to help your father and you can think this over."

Indeed, after he passed his final exams, Maxx returned to Coimbra. A feverish correspondence struck up between the two. They told each other what they were doing every day, what they were thinking, what they were feeling every single moment. As Maxx grew more and more involved in the banking industry, he would tell Ruth about numerous cases or clients he was working with. He was then almost thirty, and he hadn't done much in his life. Miriam and Anna were happily married and would soon have babies.

"I am afraid to propose to you, my sweet Ruth! I don't want to let you down. But I think I will conquer my fear, and tell you what's in my heart. I will lay my heart out into your delicate hands, and YOU, only YOU will decide!"

Ruth was certain that she loved him back, but it was hard for her to take the first step. "Coward, coward! I'm praying to God that you overcome your fear and that we can be together!" Thus ran Ruth's thoughts, Ruth with her strong but still suppressed love!

CHAPTER 11

The two of them continued writing to each other; Ruth was twenty-five and Maxx, thirty. Ruth still wondered what secret was weighing on him that he could not confess. But she had hope. Her parents no longer hoped, but let her do what she pleased. She had always been an independent and stubborn child. They had no power over that.

When Maxx turned thirty, to his surprise, the great banker Lieberman announced in front of the whole family gathered at the table that he was retiring from business.

"My dear son, I consider that you are mature enough to take over the whole business. I am tired and I will withdraw. I have admired you all these years since you have come back from the University, and I have liked your innovations. The faculty in Aveiro taught you well. Our business needs youth, new blood; and you, you are the future. You must carry on what I started when I was your age! You have only one fault, and after that, I'll say no more. You are not married! Years go by. Your mother and I are growing old, and we have no grandchildren from you. I'm thinking that you never go out; you are always wrapped up in your work, and girls cannot come into your room through the window. Only one did that, but she was not human. Have you got over her? Have you forgotten her? Did you ever get over that ordeal? You've moved to another room and locked up the old one. Are you all right? Thank God this girl is writing to you – Ruth Zuzarte, this girl who isn't getting married. I think you two match!"

"I feel better now, father, but I cannot propose to Ruth, not before I tell her my story. I have not been ready to tell her until now."

"And are you now? Can I hope for that, Maxx?"

"I think so, yes. I shall soon go to Aveiro and tell her the story. Today I am sending her a letter."

"Very well, son!"

Maxx had been planning for some time to go to Ruth's house, to talk to her and then let her decide. The older man's attitude took him by surprise, for he was letting him run the bank. Suddenly, he felt a heavy burden on his shoulders, but he knew he would be able to cope with that. He wrote to Ruth, telling her his plans. She was truly happy for him; if Maxx came to visit, that was a step towards marriage. She had nothing to forgive. The whole family in Aveiro was thrilled, and Ruth's parents were convinced that this would be a decisive visit.

"Ruth, tell us in plenty of time when he will come. We must prepare for that. It's now or never, sweetheart."

"Mother, father, please do not rush me! I will get married, but not so fast!"

"It's not fast," her father said. "I know Maxx, and his father has been my friend for a long time; I would like Maxx to be my son-in-law!"

"Please say yes, my darling. Surely he will propose to you. Do not be picky about it," Mrs. Zuzarte added.

"Oh, you are so impatient! I'm going to answer him right away. Are you happy now?"

"Yes, tell him we are waiting for him! Tell him come as soon as possible!"

What nobody knew was that the elder banker was ill, but he had been hiding that from his family for a long time. He forbade his personal doctor to mention it. He had been taking morphine for some time, but he was still in pain. He felt he would not be able to hide his illness from his family; the pain would betray him eventually. The doctor said that his days were numbered, and every sunrise was a tangible victory to him.

He knew that he would die soon, so he made a special effort, and one Sunday, he gathered all his children around the table. He was so cheerful and loving to everyone, and his two grandchildren sat on his knees tortured by pain. He cheered everyone up, including Maxx, who was usually more constrained. Nobody thought of giving an ominous meaning to the sweat on banker Lieberman's forehead; they thought it was due only to his playing with his small grandchildren.

When everybody went to their rooms for the night, the banker went upstairs, also, to his modest room, thinking to himself, "There is something special about this day! This is my last day! I shall die happy with all my family next to me. All my children are here. Why should anyone have known about it? Especially my sensitive and good wife! She wouldn't have left this room. My only sorrow is that Maxx is not married and he has no children! I hoped and hoped he would marry Ruth, but there is just friendship between them. He will go in vain to Aveiro." He said all that to himself in a quiet voice. In the past few days, when he was certain that no one could hear him, he started encouraging himself and thinking about his soul. Bitter tears flowed for the first time down the cheeks of that dying man. "I am happy! I have a wonderful family!"

In the morning, they were surprised not to see Mr. Lieberman come downstairs to say goodbye to his girls and their families, for they were leaving to go back to their homes. They found him dead in his bed. At that moment, they understood why he had asked them all to come, and why he had been so tired lately. His doctor, who came at once, felt he was freed from his promise of confidentiality, and told them everything about the illness of Mr. Lieberman. He showed them all his drawers full of pills. He took them back, for they were no good to anybody anymore.

Everybody was looking at his unmoving body, which was no longer smiling, joking, or harshly giving orders. Now Maxx had to continue the work of his father and take care of the funeral. The women, as he knew very well, were not able to do that. He took the carriage and made all the arrangements for proper ceremony. Flowers, a suitable coffin, and everything else that was needed. He announced his father's death at City Hall and signed everything that had to be signed; then, exhausted, he went back home.

His father's body was laid in the entrance hall so that anyone who wanted to pay their last respects could do so. He was to be buried the following day. After that, Maxx wrote to Ruth about the tragic event and asked her and her family to pay them a visit. Surely, Maxx wrote, they wouldn't be able to attend the funeral, but their presence would comfort the family if they wanted to come.

People came from the village, when they learned the news. People brought flowers, many flowers. The last flowers for Mr. Lieberman. They were trying to comfort the family, shaking hands all around, and then, in silence, they returned home.

The next day, when the coffin was to be placed into the dust that we all return to at some point, it rained. That was a bleak day after all that rain. People in the village whispered that it was a sign, that maybe the banker was sad wherever he was then, and yet reconciled. The funeral didn't last long because of the rain, but what difference did that make? The strong, brave man could never return to his family. Mrs. Rosa, her daughters on either side, was like a marble statue. What a kind man! He did not want her to suffer. He did not let her know about his illness so that she would not agonize along with him. He had written her a letter, a goodbye letter, wherein he reminded her of their youth and their happy marriage. He begged her to be calm and serene, and he promised to wait for her. Then he said, "Maybe you will live to see Maxx get married and settled down, but try and remember every detail, because I will ask you all about it!" Mr. Lieberman left letters for each of his children, brief but full of kindness and fatherly love. He had passed away, so they had to learn to accept it and live without him.

When Ruth received Maxx's letter, she jumped with joy and happiness, but then as she read each line, her beautiful face became twisted in obvious sadness. Tears ran past her long eyelashes.

"Father, Mister Lieberman passed away! He hid his suffering and his illness from his family. Nobody knew anything about it. He was buried yesterday. Maxx has written to me inviting us to the castle, for he is tired and he needs me."

"What a tragedy, my sweetheart, but I cannot go! You go with your mother; I can see clearly that you will get married after the mourning. I have no doubt about that. Pack your bags, for tomorrow morning you will be leaving. You must keep me posted about everything. Lieberman was my friend, and I shall be Maxx's father from now on. I shall write a letter to Maxx, and you Ruth, get ready for your wedding! It will be a simple one, without glamor, as you wish it to be."

"Now I know that, father! Maxx will ask me to marry him."

"And I am getting rid of you so elegantly, my dear, but the occasion is so sad," Mr. Zuzarte laughed, though it was edged with grief.

"It is not important; my being married to Maxx will give me the chance to help him and support him always and forever, and I think that is the most important thing of all!"

The next morning, the Zuzartes' carriage set off to Coimbra, but Ruth was not interested this time in the woods, or birds; it seemed they would never reach their destination.

"When will we get there?" she asked over and over.

"Relax. You are so agitated! You must be calm for Maxx! Have you forgotten that?"

"Yes, you're right."

When they finally arrived, the Liebermans received them with all their love, especially Maxx and Mrs. Rosa. The girls were preparing to leave with their husbands, who had business to take care of and other chores that could not be postponed. In fact, their life was flowing like their beloved river, for one cannot sit in one place and think the same things over and over again. Even if one is wrapped up in thoughts, after a while, those thoughts will stop having any effect. Maxx took Ruth by the hand, and the two mothers walked behind them.

"I thought I would never get here! The road seemed so long!"

"I know what you mean!" Maxx said. "I was going over your journey in my mind, thinking where you might be."

After the women made themselves comfortable in their rooms, they came downstairs for dinner. They expressed their condolences and regrets on behalf of the Zuzartes, asking them to accept Mr. Zuzarte's apologies for not coming, because of his obligations at the University as well as his other business. Then Ruth gave Maxx the letter from her father. He opened it and read it.

"What a wonderful man your father is!"

"I shall write to him every day; I promised I would keep him posted," Ruth said.

"That's very nice of you, very nice indeed," Mrs. Rosa added. She told them that her late husband, in his goodbye letter to her, had forbidden her to be sad after he was gone. "So I must do what he asked! I have always listened to him, and that was a good thing to do! But I miss him; I have his things, the memories... and then, I have Maxx."

"I think you are right," Mrs. Zuzarte said. One should carry one's sorrow in one's soul with dignity, and show that to the world."

"That's right...."

After dinner, the ladies wanted to rest. Maxx seized the opportunity to stop Ruth for a second.

"It can't be done right now, because you are tired, but tomorrow I would like to talk to you, to make a confession to you. And after that, if you will still want me, I will propose to you. I cannot offer you an engagement party, as you can well see."

"But that doesn't matter to me," Ruth exclaimed, taking his hand. "I don't want any party!" Maxx held her close for a long time, aware of her fragrance surrounding him.

"Thank you, Ruth," Maxx said, lightly touching her cheek with his lips. Ruth squeezed his hand, the closed her eyes.

"We'll talk tomorrow, then. Good night!"

"Good night, my darling!"

Maxx remained downstairs, watching Ruth climb the stairs. Only good God knows how the two young people slept, but the truth is that both of them waited impatiently for the morning when just the two of them would be together. From her window, Ruth could see the park and the small cottage by the gate. After breakfast, their mothers left for a walk in the park. Maxx stopped Ruth in the parlor, and spoke to her candidly.

"Ruth, I love you very much, differently than I loved before. But, to have you as my wife, I must tell you everything, I must be honest with you. It is difficult for me, but I will tell you my story."

"I love you too, Maxx! Tell me what it is that you have on your heart; be free, and set yourself free, so you can fly!"

"I have not been engaged before, as I told you, but I did love, only it was an impossible love, a hopeless love, for I loved a soul from another world!"

Bit by bit, Maxx told her everything about his encounter with Lucia, about Lucia and her life.

"Everybody sustained me and helped me, and I mean the whole village. It was after that, that I decided to choose another room for myself, and to go to study in Aveiro."

"And that was a wise thing to do, Maxx; otherwise you would not have met me!"

"So... how is it going to be? I need you," Maxx summed up, "and I don't want to let you down, not even a little!"

"Maxx, the past doesn't change the future in any way, and I do want to marry you! We will always help each other, won't we!"

"Then, may I put the engagement ring on your finger?"

"Yes, absolutely!"

Maxx took a small, elegant box from his pocket. It held a ring which he tenderly slipped onto Ruth's ring finger. Then he took her in his arms and swung her all around the room. They were both laughing, and their laughter drew the other ladies into the parlor.

"Mother, we are engaged! Look!" Floating with happiness, Ruth showed her mother the ring.

"I am so glad for both of you," Mrs. Lieberman said joyfully. "Now your father is present here, too! This is such a happy moment! My husband doesn't allow us to be sad. We have all the time in the world to prepare the wedding. We will hold it in the park, using that enormous altar that my girls used. Would you like to have a big wedding, Ruth?"

"No, not at all! I just want Maxx, whom I am now asking to show me the park."

"Then we ladies must keep each other company. Would you like some tea, Mrs. Zuzarte?"

"Yes, I am tired after that outing. A cup of tea right now would be perfect, and it would refresh me after so much walking. It is indeed a splendid park!"

"It is indeed."

Their wedding took place after the mourning period ended, and it was simple, with nothing elaborate. The young couple looked radiant under their wedding canopy, for they had each other; and when Maxx broke the glasses for good luck, he looked upstairs and saw Lucia blessing them. "I will be happy! Now I can live in peace!" Then he lovingly kissed his wife.

The newly married couple decided to live in the castle. They were joyful and renewed. They mutually helped and completed each other, and once their baby was born, the shadows of the past that had darkened Maxx's forehead disappeared completely. Their love showed that with patience one can indeed surmount any obstacle. Their life ran smoothly, just like their dear river, the Mondego.

The castle was still occupied, but nobody ever troubled their peace again.

EPILOGUE

Do you believe in ghosts? What about positive and negative energies? I believe that the departed souls remain with us in some way or another. They linger close to their home. Most of them are peaceful; others need to be helped by different means or methods to find their peace. Some ghosts are pleasant and friendly. It all comes down to our preconceived ideas about them and the channel through which some of us have the possibility to be open to a world parallel to ours. There are ghosts who love their new friends, and others that do not have feelings.

Could you love a ghost? Or is this just a fantasy?

The End

February, 2012

The following novels written by the same author were published also by Infarom Publishing:

"Once I was King"
"A Butterfly with Burning Wings"